Bothering the Coffee Drinkers

Bothering the Coffee Drinkers

Musical Fiction and Essays

by

Doug Hoekstra

CANOPIC
PUBLISHING

Gatlinburg, Tennessee

Canopic Publishing
1843 Hidden Hills Rd
Gatlinburg, TN 37738
www.canopicpublishing.com

Book design by Phil Rice
Cover design by Joe Montgomery/Wednesday Design
Cover photo © Bryan Mullennix/Photodisc Red

Library of Congress Cataloging-in-Publication Data

Hoekstra, Doug, 1962-
  Bothering the coffee drinkers : musical fiction and essays / by
Doug
Hoekstra.— 1st ed.
     p. cm.
   ISBN-13: 978-0-9728604-4-4 (alk. paper)
   ISBN-10: 0-9728604-4-4 (alk. paper)
   I. Title.

   PS3608.O476B68 2006
   813'.6—dc22

                                                  2006002799

Printed in the United States of America
10 9 8 7 6 5 4 3 2 1
First Edition

Acknowledgments and Special Thanks

Bothering the Coffee Drinkers: Musical Fiction and Essays is a collection of stories informed by my experiences negotiating the realm of the under-the-radar independent artist. While it is true that I have been a performing singer-songwriter for some years now, these are fictions, save for the two memoir pieces that sandwich the collection, the idea being to start the reader off in reality, and fade into the imagined world much like an episode of *Gilligan's Island* or some such pop culture dreamscape, only to return back to reality at the end. Along the way, the tales, while not strictly autobiographical, do flow from the places I've been and people I've met, be they peers, friends, strangers. My intention is that while the characters are sometimes faced with trying or bizarre circumstances, there remains a sense of hope and resolution that runs through the book, as these modern day musical impressionists work to appreciate what they've been dealt and continue to persevere in search of a better day—all for the sake of the song. This book is for all those artists, weak and strong, barreling across your country right now.

I'd also like to thank everyone who read some or all of these stories in various forms. Early on, Allan Carter offered encouragement; Cliff Goldmacher and Sandra Smith Hutchins were diligent readers; Joe Montgomery whipped up a tall latte of a cover design; and Phil Rice provided valuable feedback and of course, brought the book to fruition. Thanks also to my wife Molly Hoekstra, for her love and close reading, and my son Jude, for helping me see these stories and the world at large in a different, better way.

Finally, some of these stories appeared in various forms in previous publications and thanks go to the following for stoking the furnace: *The Palo Alto Review* ("The Blarney Stone"), *Pure Music* ("Bothering the Coffeedrinkers"), *Si Senor* ("Billy and the Tuba"), *Sugar Mule* ("The Town Crier"), and *Southern Hum* ("Kudzu").

Hope you enjoy the read,

Doug Hoekstra, Nashville, 2006

Contents

Bothering the Coffee Drinkers

The Blarney Stone (a true story)

Our yard stretches out in front of an old bungalow on a shady street in one of Nashville's few historic districts. There's a plaque on the five-point junction around the corner, which tells you that the trolley cars used to run here back in the twenties. I'm not sure how long our house has been there, but there are huge elm trees in the front yard that are very close to the porch and rise up to pass the upstairs window, right past our attic, higher and higher, "up to the moon," as I tell my son.

Just the other night I spent a lot of time running around those trees, going in circles. It was a beautiful summer evening, about seven p.m., with a little bit of dusk falling in the sky and a soft breeze blowing across the yard. My little boy and I were having a good time of it, playing "throw the ball," and "peekaboo." "More Daddy, Daddy funny" Jude shouted and laughed, as I ran around one tree, across the sidewalk, around the other and up on the porch. Huffing and puffing, on it went, I had to pace myself, but in the end, I knew I'd die to make his life better than mine. But, as the sweat running down my back cooled me, I reminded myself that this fatherhood thing was a marathon, not a sprint, and as fun as this was, there were lots more to come.

Jude must have sensed my thoughts, for as I jumped, dashed, and bolted one last time, he stood up and got off the front steps, feet first, as we've taught him. Then, his legs worked it, small steps catapulted with great speed, waddling forward as he pointed his finger into the air. He held a small letter "j" in the other hand and shouted, "J goes Jah." He was 18 months old, but already with a firm mind of his own, and as I watched him, I realized he was running off to make "weeshes." Through the grass he went, "grassy grass," he said, pointing at his shoes, "big boy shoes," came the utterance, and finally, he reached a dandelion worthy of a weesh. He reached down to pick it up and snatched it from the ground. Then he handed it to me, saying "weeshes." This is the signal that I'm supposed to blow the seeds into the air. But, first I asked, "what do you want to wish for, Jude?" And, he said "Daddy." And so, I blew, he laughed, and the seeds shot into the still air, falling lightly on the grass, where they will take root again, and ultimately, turn into more wishes. "More weeshes," he shouted, "more weeshes."

Later that night, I ventured into the junk room for some clean-up work. The junk room is one of two low-ceilinged loft rooms upstairs. Sometimes the junk room is also called the music room or the writing room, depending on how I'm trying to feed my ego and make a few extra bucks that particular week. If you head up our cat-fur-in-fested stairs and turn left, you'll find a jumbled array of stuff worthy of any good pack rat. There's my portable recording studio, an old Wurlitzer piano, and an electric guitar in the corner. A picnic basket my parents used to use when they were courting sits under the piano and is filled with an array of cords and microphones. A shelf full of old LPs and 45s sits against the opposite wall, covered with Beatles memorabilia given to me over the years. Next to it, a wooden cabinet full of cassettes and DAT tapes of old gigs, and next to that, our back-up computer, which sits on a hassock that is filled with old Chicago Cubs programs. Throughout the room there are filing cabinets—they are filled with tax receipts, old writings, press clips, playbills, school diplomas and transcripts, and the like. And, in the remaining corner, there are about ten boxes of junk I've been meaning to clear out of there ever since we moved in. Junk in neat little black and white boxes, that fold-up kind you buy at Office Max, each one labeled with a sharpie pen, junk preceded by the appropriate adjective.

Four of them read "Photo Junk."

I don't know how I got to be such a picture taker, I guess it goes back to my family roots, my dad's cameras and home movie projectors. Christmas morning with flood-lights felt like Hollywood sometimes and heated us up enough to catch a tan and I'm exaggerating, but only slightly. Each year, kodachrome shots of the birthday cake, the opening of the gifts, and my brother's latest girlfriend in the back-ground, you could bind them all and make a flipbook. Since then, technology has improved and the video cam and the

APS pocket camera are so lightweight and portable, I suppose that only contributes to the abundance of documentation. As a photographer, I never really get too technical; I just snap away and try to treat my subject in an interesting fashion. Turn the camera a little, get a vibe, put the subject at the side and frame something interesting going on behind—nothing fancy, really. I used to be very diligent about getting our still prints developed and into photo albums immediately, arranging them along with ticket stubs and program stubs, and clippings from the newspaper, little bound collages, personal works of art, to be viewed at some later date, by me, Molly, or, someday, our child. Sometimes I'd romanticize about whose eyes would see those books.

As time went on, however, and particularly after we got married, our busy lives got busier, and the memories piled up and didn't get into the albums and before you knew it, I couldn't be bothered, I was too far behind. From time to time, I'd think about catching up but always put it off. This was symbolic, in a sense, as if we were living a life where our past had some meaning, the present was everything and the future, well, who knew? Several people told me our lives would change forever once our child came onto the scene, and they were so right, in so many ways, all positive, many that I could have never imagined. As the future took shape, its significance was reinforced, and underscored.

Of course, to move into the future, you've got to clean up your past. I picked a photo box at random, opened the lid and sifted through some papers and programs and itineraries that covered the pictures below. It was Photo Junk Box 2 and it didn't take me long to identify it as the box belonging to a European tour I did in the fall of 2001. This was a five-week jaunt to promote a new record released on a Dutch label. I left out of Chicago O'Hare on October 11th (amidst National Guard reserves in the airports and national terrorist paranoia in full-force) and landed across the pond, in Amsterdam Schiphol (amidst a nation riding around on bicycles, well-oiled, and relaxed). After the Netherlands, the itinerary took me by train to London, by car up to Scotland, and on the ferry over to Ireland. It was rough being away from Molly for that long, but fortunately she was embroiled in student teaching at the time, very busy, and the timing for us and opportunities for the new record looked good. As I sorted through maps of London and Edinburgh and Dublin, tube tickets, and handbills for my shows, I remembered the anticipation mixed with the dread, and the successes measured with the occasional disappointments. All my tours have been like that, really.

After digging past the souvenir papers, I reached the first sheaf of photos, opened up the "24-hour processing" envelope and looked inside. Shuffling through the stack, I saw shots of Ireland, the Blarney Castle, me kissing the Blarney Stone, the wishing pond, the stairs leading down from the castle, and the destinations that followed—Cobh, Clonakilty Cork, and Dublin. Ireland was the least enjoyable part of that particular tour, only because it was at the end of a very busy and tiring itinerary. The Irish leg was short and there was very little time to sightsee, the Blarney Castle being one of the exceptions. It was located right off the N20 between Limerick and Cobh, which gave me enough time for a quick looksee on my drive down, before my soundcheck at the Sirius Arts Centre.

My anticipation for this Castle visit had been great, not only because it was a rare chance to do something on my own time, but because the drive from Limerick took an inordinate amount of that precious time, roads twisting and turning and winding, speed limits going up and down like hummingbirds. Nothing like the M1 in England or Autobahn of Germany, Irish roads are like the backroads that take one through the small towns of Wisconsin or Iowa once you venture away from the neverland of the U.S. Interstate. When I was growing up in Chicago, I used to romanticize over the loss of the back roads in the states, but then I started playing music and became enamored of getting places quicker. Lately, I've been taking my time again, but that's another story.

Most folks have heard of the Blarney Stone, but whenever I talk about it with someone, I've found that there's some difference of opinion as to what can be had from kissing the fabled rock. Some say you get a wish; others say it makes you more eloquent. In modern lingo, it can give the kisser the "gift of gab" or if you go back to the 18th century, a French consul said you "gain the privilege of telling lies for seven years." And, one must check in with Queen Elizabeth I, who reportedly coined the phrase "blarney" due to her frustration at Lord Blarney's ability to talk endlessly without ever actually agreeing to her demands. My feeling is that in the end, kissing the Blarney Stone is like a lot of things—the kisser is the judge, it is your experience, and you get out of it what you put into it.

After bearing with the N20 through all the twists and turns, I made it to Blarney Castle around 3:30 in the afternoon on a brisk November afternoon. The seasons were changing, and the airs were getting cooler, and the days were getting shorter. Leaving my "motor in a car park," I walked past the souvenir shop and paid my admission. Then, I passed through the gate and onto the grounds of the castle, which are deeply green, picturesque, and tranquil. The River Martin winds through the quiet, past pear, beech, and evergreen oaks. Over yonder I saw a druid circle of stones called the Rock Close, which included a sacrificial altar and a witches kitchen, conjuring up visions of Macbeth. But darkness wasn't far from coming on and the grounds would be closing soon, so I skipped the brew and hurried over the wooden bridge and up the grassy hill, to the entrance of the castle. I walked with big paces, and then ran a little bit, and soon I was there.

The Blarney Castle began life as a hunting lodge in the 10th century, the castle itself being a tower house that was built five centuries later. The Blarney Stone is believed to be half of the Stone of Scone, which was originally a possession of the Scots. The other half is in Edinburgh Castle, where coincidentally or not, I'd visited just before taking the ferry to Ireland. Robert the Bruce gave the stone to Cormac McCarthy in return for his support in the Battle of Bannockburn. Legend has it that Scottish Kings were crowned over the stone because it was believed to have special powers.

What I didn't know until I entered the castle was that the stone itself sits high up in the battlements, and I'd need to draw on some of those special powers to get to the top. I'm terribly afraid of heights, particularly on staircases or ledges with open spaces. Once I entered the castle, the dusky light that had been blanketing the grounds vanished, replaced by an abrupt blackness. I stopped for a second to let my eyes adjust and my dark glasses lighten. I looked up and realized it was going to be tough going; in front of me was an endless row of narrow stone steps heading up, up, up. The staircases in this castle were built to be intentionally narrow and steep so only one invader at a time could come up the steps. And the windows were very narrow, which darkened the interior but also provided defense, so arrows couldn't come in from the outside.

On the other hand, windows helped close in the space a bit, which gave me a little psychological security and a boost to continue upward and into the black. I thought back to the time I'd been to the Statue of Liberty in New York and hung out at the base of the structure, stopped by fear from venturing up to the torch. Or the time my family visited the Gateway Arch in St. Louis and my mother started telling all the other tourists in the observation deck that the structure was swaying. Or the time I was supposed to go to the top of the Sears Tower in Chicago while my brother went to the top of the Hancock Center, the plan being to get on the observation decks and wave to each other through the quarter-run telescopes. I never made it off the elevator. This time, however, my plan wouldn't fail. Destiny was nebulous to me, yet I felt strangely destined to make it up those rickety stairs to the top, to rise up, so to speak, and kiss the fabled stone. It was a mission, something greater than a much welcome break from my incessant tour movements. So, I wet my lips, put my head down, and raced up those stairs as fast as my knees could take me, slight flashes of light piercing the darkness whenever a window passed me by.

Magic or coincidence, I don't know, but all these thoughts rifled through my head like a deck of cards and the next thing I knew I'd made it to the top of the castle without fainting, throwing up, or retreating. As the staircase ended, I stumbled into the open air, a stone clearing of sorts, with no ceiling or high walls to hold me in. Catching my breath, I stopped still and saw green fields below stretched out across the land and to the gate from whence I came. Beyond that, the village of Blarney was visible on the distant horizon. And, directly across from where I was standing, two men were congregating around what appeared to be the stone itself. One fellow looked to be a tourist; he stood up, dusted himself off, and adjusted his fanny pack, moving his butt back and forth, tugging on his shorts. He was a bit overweight and sure enough, as I moved closer, I could see his T-shirt read "University of Indiana." He handed an attendee a couple of coins and walked towards my direction, following a path laid out along the edge of the castle roof. The walkway was very narrow, so I waited for him to pass me and start heading down the stairway before I slowly moved towards the stone, staying as far inside as I possibly could.

Now, for those of you who haven't been, once you reach the stone, you notice that there is a sizeable gap between where the surface ends and the top of the wall begins, and the stone is embedded at the top of that wall. The stone is also a little bit below the surface, so what you do is, you lay down on your back, grab two iron bars that run parallel to the wall, lean your head backwards, upside down, in order to kiss the stone. In other words, you're literally bending over backwards, and lowering yourself about two feet below floor level. If you open your eyes (which I wasn't about to do), you see straight through the space to the fields below. And, if this doesn't make you nervous enough, before getting in position, you're instructed to remove all beads, bracelets, glasses, and bodily decorations, lest they go flying off into space.

The other fellow I'd seen turned out to be the attendant, a middle-aged man with sandy hair, blue jeans and a tan work jacket. He could've been the ticket taker or he could've been the maintenance man or he could've been the tour guide. Yet, today, he was the keeper of the stone. He welcomed me, smiling ever so slightly as I handed him my glasses and my camera. I wondered if my face was white, and I thought about what a terrible bungee jumper I'd be if I ever wound up touring New Zealand, and I formed a wish in my head to hold onto before and during my kiss. I knew about the eloquence bit, but I figured I'd better have a wish handy, just in case, why waste it, right? And, if you're wondering, well, I wasn't casting my lot with a wish for a bungee-free future, a safe walk back down the staircase, or a return trip to the Gateway Arch. Boring wishes, those would be. And, for those who really know me, I wasn't going to wish that the Cubs would win the World Series the following year, though I must admit that one crossed my mind briefly.

My wish actually came to me quickly, so I dropped down on the mat that's laid out on the stone floor, grabbed the bars, and felt the attendant's hands hold onto my midsection as I lowered my head. He held me firmly in place as I smacked the stone with my lips. He pulled one hand off right as I did so, which gave me a start, until the flash on my camera went off. He's got to be good at this, and that's why we tip him—he's responsible for our jewelry, lives, and photographic memories. He's not only the keeper of the stone; he's the keeper of the stories. If I'd fallen, there would've been perfect documentation for family and friends back home. Feeling powerful and brave, but also thankful it was over, I shook his hand and dropped a fiver in his tip jar. He nodded a thank you, took a rag from a little doctor's bag he had with him, and began wiping the stone clean.

As it turned out, no one else was waiting behind me, so I must have been the last kisser of the day, which no doubt would lend extra value to my wish. Indeed, he could wipe the stone off, but unless vandals snuck onto the ground, there wouldn't be another wish until the next morning. And so I retraced my steps, heading down to the castle base and out onto the grounds with a spring in my heart. Stopping for a second on the footbridge over the river, I looked into the water and saw dozens of coins lying at the bottom. I fished a two pence coin out of my pocket, wound up, and threw it a little further behind where most of the coins congregated. Up high in the air it went, arcing almost to the point where the moon was beginning to glimmer through the trees, low in the sky. It splashed into the water, rippling over my meditation.

It was the same wish on this coin that I'd laid on the stone, and if you're wondering, well, no, I wasn't about to put my wish around a million bucks, that just wasn't in me. And, I didn't go for my own reality show, world peace, or eternal life. No, instead I settled on something that I hoped would be as real as any wish could be, a wish that while not a trick wish, could still bring even more wishes. It was also a wish that would probably take a little time to come true, once I got back to the States and help put events in motion, which would be part of the fun of it all. So, I filed that wish for future reference.

As I was reliving all these thoughts with pictures in hand, my son woke from his nap in the next room, and came waddling in, tousled hair, and a slightly confused look on his face. "Hi Daddy," he said, and then began pointing again. "Daddy guitar," he said, directing his finger at the electric in the corner. "Boogaloo."

"Okay, Jude," I replied, putting the photos away and picking up the instrument. I started to play a little 12-bar deal with poorly improvised lyrics centering around, you guessed it, the hook phrase "do the boogaloo." He rocked up and down, in what he calls a "dancing break."

Of course he'd like to dance. After all, my son's full name is Jude Aaron Hoekstra. I must let you know, however, that the Jude bit did not come from the Beatles song, so don't start singing it, like everyone who meets him does. Ironically, when he was about three months old, after listening to a friend give us our 3,762nd accapella version of "Hey Jude," I suddenly remembered that was the first song I'd ever performed in front of an audience, back at my eighth grade talent show. But, who would name their son after that? Certainly not me.

And, before you ask the second question everyone asks, I must tell you that the Jude bit did not come from St. Jude, the patron saint of lost causes. That said, I've been in more than my share of taxis in my day, and it seems I see St.

Jude on the dash as much as Jesus or St. Christopher. And, dig this, when my son was five months old, I was strumming my guitar, running through some old material for a show, and remembered an old song I wrote called "Slipping Through the Cracks," where I sing "St. Jude be my patron saint, deliver me while I wait." But who would name their son after one of his own song lyrics? Certainly not me. But I have thought about these signposts after the fact. Were they magic or coincidence? I wondered, and I pass that query along to you.

In the end, Molly and I sum it all up by saying that he was named Jude because we liked the way it sounded, it's a classic name, and it sounded good with Hoekstra. As for Aaron, well, that's a nod to our favorite king, the one that used to live in Memphis, and if you throw in the fact that the initials spell Jah and Jah is high praise in both Germany and Jamaica, well, it all comes together, doesn't it? J goes Jah. As anyone with children will tell you, once they are born and named, you can't imagine them being anything else. He is a perfect Jude, and I thought that from the moment he made it onto the scene.

Jude was expected to come in late October and so we figured he'd be a Libra boy. But, he had his own ideas about things, and as the leaves began to fall and the World Series came and went, we started to get into Scorpio territory with still no sign of his arrival. Our doctor, who looks and acts weirdly like David Letterman, had set a date for an appointment with us to decide whether he needed to go in and get him, so to speak. But, on the day before that appointment, at 6 a.m. on a cool autumn morning, Molly woke me and showed me where our futon had been soaked through, as if someone had emptied a gallon drum of water on it. The moment had come. She called the hospital and they told us to wait about four hours, and then come on in. We set the alarm and went back to sleep on the floor.

Around 10 a.m., we set out for the hospital, stopping at the Mapco down the street for the Sunday paper and some snacks. Looking back, it's strange how it was all so mellow and methodical. I guess I'd expected something more like an old Dick Van Dyke or Fred Flintstone episode where, as the man in the family, I'd be running around shouting like a crazy person, stuffing nightgowns and slippers into overnight bags, while my wife sat calmly waiting for me to escort her to the car. It wasn't like that at all. It was all measured, and after all, the hospital was only five blocks away, so once we got there and checked in, we began the rest of what would be the 24-hour show of a lifetime. All I can say about that is I don't know how women do it; if it were up to men, we'd never repopulate this world—we simply couldn't take it. Molly was amazingly focused, physically and mentally, as slowly the past burned away and the future came upon us as our little boy inched his way into the world.

Sadly, David Letterman hadn't been on duty that morning, so we were left with his colleague, a younger doctor who was extremely efficient and businesslike, albeit less jovial. Every hour, he'd come in, ask the nurse on duty about the epidural, check the clipboard at the foot of the bed, and make a notation. Then he'd stand silently, with one hand on his hip and the other extended, like a modern dancer in scrubs. And, like a partner in the dance, the nurse would run over and put a surgical glove on the free hand, pulling it tight upon his wrist. All spruced up, in he'd go, checking things out and making sure Jude was on schedule, descending a little bit each hour. Then he'd pull out, hold up his hand, and the nurse would remove the glove. He'd make another notation and leave the nurse to continue with the coaching, checking and mopping up of the amniotic fluid, which by early morning was literally pouring onto the floor.

It wasn't until about 5 a.m. that Jude, in the last possible hour of delivery before we'd still have to go in and get him, with a mind of his own even then, was finally, truly ready to come on down. There was a small crowd on hand by now, an extra nurse helping with the pushing, two nurses setting up the incubator, the anesthesiologist checking in and finally, the doctor, here to stay this time. He pulled up his stool and got ready to grab the glory, so to speak. Basically, throughout the evening and early morning, things like "good job" came out of my mouth in shades of regularity while I held Molly's hand and lent my moral support. But the truth was I was in awe, dumbstruck by her grace under pressure and the whole experience of seeing something happen that's never happened to you before, overwhelming to the point where it instantly becomes one of the things you'll think about on your deathbed. And all my words stopped as I saw the top of his head poke into view, all words subdued by a laugh that was equally tears of joy. He had a good head of hair for a newborn and the nurse suggested we reach down and feel it. I did so, but Molly passed, because true to form, she just wanted to keep on pushing. The doctor thought Jude might need a little help, so he got out the vacuum and told us that on the next push he was going to give a little tug. Here we go, get ready, he timed it, 1,2,3, Molly pushed hard and out he came in one big motion, all arms and legs, POOF, Jude was here. The doctor held him up, he looked straight at me, seemingly clear and focused, as if to say, "Hello, Dad."

The cord was cut, and he was carried to his mother, where he latched on immediately and began feeding. In five seconds, my entire perception of the world had changed, for when I saw my son's face, an old proverb popped into my head. "There was never a time when you or I did not exist. Nor will there be any future when we shall cease to be." I couldn't remember where I'd heard that, but it perfectly summed what I had seen in my son's eyes. Later, I looked up the quote and it turned out to be from the Bhagavad-Gita, a long way from our little hospital room to my heart, but it was also indicative of how great distances had suddenly now become much closer.

The next day I made a few calls from the hospital. After family, I got in touch with the folks at Hatch Show Print, who were in the process of putting together a stylish ink-pressed birth announcement for us. We'd already talked about specs, and I'd given them his name ahead of time, but now the details needed to be filled in. Congratulations came upon answer, and I continued with 5:49 a.m., 8 lb., 15 oz., 22 inches. Then the girl at the shop asked me, "and what date was it, today?"

"Oh yes, of course, how could I forget," I said, elated but sleep deprived. "This morning, so that's November 4, 2002."

After I hung up the phone, I thought about that.

Throughout our years together, I've fallen into a strange habit of commenting to Molly on things from the calendar, like "hey, a week ago today we went to Cheekwood" or "a month ago today my folks were in town," or "six months ago we were on our way to New Mexico." She humors me, but I must say in some simple way, it fascinates me, as if time doesn't really move from here to there, but around us, because often memories are so vivid they feel as if they are recurring like so many points of a circle, revolving endlessly. And, so those numbers, with that year, lingered with me. I pulled open the journal I'd brought with me to take notes on the delivery and I paged backward, and as I did so, the focus became sharper and I remembered something that happened exactly a year before, flat on my back on the top of the Blarney Castle.

Magic or coincidence?

I'll leave that for you to decide. But I've got my answer.

That's the thing about Jude, he always asks for more wishes, and who can argue with that? He came on a wish and brought wishes back into our lives. Someday we'll all go to the Blarney Stone together, and I'll show him where I walked, and I'll pass my wish along to him. I know he'll use it well.

Bothering the Coffee Drinkers

Johnny Q was bothering the coffee drinkers again, a ritual he thought he'd left on the shoulder of his past, before his career had risen to that indefinable next level. It was something he'd sworn off, and yet like a junkie who is lost without a good methadone clinic, Johnny Q had backslid into an old bad habit. So, there he stood in the corner, one knee gently moving to a self-imposed beat, playing a song from his latest album, a song he had performed on National Public Radio, a song that was favorably reviewed in Billboard magazine, a song he'd played in front of crowds in clubs from in L.A to New York, and even across the pond in Paris, a song that had wound up in an independent film that played on the Sundance Channel from time to time—it starred that chick who used to date that guy in the White Stripes. But the patrons in front of him were oblivious to this song's short yet storied history; to them, it was another song played by another man with a guitar. There were always guys and girls with guitars on Sunday afternoon, and maybe some coffee drinkers would come up to him afterwards and tell him about the songs *they* wrote and how they'd once had a band before they decided to start their software company.

Although it had been a couple years since he swore off these types of shows, thinking they were behind him, everything quickly came back to Johnny Q. It was always the same, the little café in the corner of the bookstore, with the scattered tables and comfy sofa, the battered P.A. that got wheeled out of the backroom by the clerk at the counter, who also brought forth milk crates full of tangled cords. Once Johnny Q set the thing up, no mean trick because the bookstore clerk never had a clue and would always leave him on his own, the P.A. would hum and click and sometimes pick up police calls from passing CB radios. Johnny Q always positioned the two speakers on either side of his makeshift stage, positioning them on high chairs normally reserved for toddlers.

As Johnny Q began playing, he saw an all-too familiar cast of characters trickling through the front door of the bookstore. Soon there would be a little girl in pigtails about five years old dancing in the front, smiling and running back to her mom who sat nearby, reading a copy of *Redbook* and generally ignoring both the child and the music. Next to her at the table would be her husband, face buried in a Something for Dummies book, rocking the two-year-old sibling, who was sitting in a stroller with pacifier stuffed into the mouth. They looked permanently distracted, these parents, and much too tired to clap.

Behind them there would be a table or two of college kids, reading books and magazines they didn't want to buy, talking amongst themselves, sometimes louder than the performer, oblivious to where one song ended and another began. Despite their propensity to save money by not buying books or records, they always seemed to be sipping expensive triple lattes and double espressos and, between that and the conversation, were always too self-focused and wound up too clap.

Scattered here and there would be a couple 50-something men with grey in their beards and yellow in their sweaters, reading sports magazines, aimlessly licking their index fingers, turning pages, occasionally looking up with a startled reminder that there was music in front of them, finally awakening to their surroundings by the time the next song began, and, as such, they were usually too late to clap. These gentlemen were also the most likely to come up to him between sets and tell him about the bluegrass band they'd seen at some festival, mighty good pickers, they were.

There was always a single mom in shorts, looking tired but happy with a small child in lap, sitting together on the comfy sofa in the back. She'd read softly to the drooling offspring, glancing up occasionally for a weak nod or smile in the direction of the stage directly ahead. Her hands were full with book and child, and, as such, she usually just kept reading, occasionally quickly slapping a palm against the thigh in a vain attempt to clap, which was courteous, he must admit.

There was always a gaggle of customers of all ages by the magazine stands beyond the single mom, outside of the café area, leafing through this and that, pretending not to listen at all, polishing their cool, it seemed. They were definitely drawn by the music, though, because they would generally stand there the entire set before leaving, sometimes putting down a magazine long enough to throw out a few golf claps.

Finally there was always an elderly man or woman who would sit up front, with a hardcover book, usually something classic. Johnny Q would read the titles during the instrumental breaks in his songs, and more often than not, this person would put down Fitzgerald or Hemingway, make solid eye contact with him, eyes faded in color yet gracious in their manner. Invariably, these people always clapped the loudest.

And, sure enough, as Johnny Q looked out on the small crowd, while picking the tune that was receiving all the praise in consciousnesses beyond those of the coffee drinkers he was bothering, this is what he saw. He tried desperately to concentrate on the music he was playing. Because if he didn't, he'd start wondering why he'd agreed to do this show, and then the negativity would seep through his fingers, cause his hands to stumble and his mind to forget words to songs he'd sung a thousand times. It's difficult to play off a crowd that isn't there; it's worse than hecklers, he thought. At least a heckler gives you something to work with. As he finished the song, blasts of espresso machine followed, and car engines revved in the parking lot behind the corner of glass behind him.

The parking lot behind him belonged to Greensboro, North Carolina, just across the interstate from Winston-Salem, an old tobacco town that used to be, and somewhere between laid-back Asheville and the booming Research Triangle, where he was playing the next night. It was a Sunday afternoon, and these factors combined to form the reason why he was there. Sundays were typically tough days to fill, and he'd decided, in a moment of foolishness, that any money would be better than no money. So, it was all because of routing, the Justification of the Week. After Chapel Hill on Monday, it was Richmond on Tuesday, Washington on Wednesday, and then to New York. Johnny Q told his manager, as they planned the shows, that he'd rather be playing than not playing, and after all, it was a new market.

"Yeah, the first time through is great," said his manager, "and so is the eighth. It's the six times in-between that kill you."

After the first set, Johnny Q grabbed a magazine and then snuck off to the CD department to spend his gift certificate, which he received on top of his small guarantee. Johnny Q searched in vain for the counter display of his new release, which the store had promised to set up at least one week before the show. He handed his items to the clerk, a young man with a crew cut and a piercing just above his right eyebrow.

"Sounded pretty good," the clerk said, scanning Johnny's purchases.

"You could hear it over here?" Johnny Q asked.

"They pipe it in," the clerk said. "Do you know Silas Henderson?"

"No I don't." Silas was a peer, another singer-songwriter in the game. They'd shared a bill once, some little club in Birmingham, spent a few minutes talking about guitar strings in-between sets.

"He was here Friday night," the clerk added. "The place was *packed out.*"

The past few days Johnny Q noticed they'd been doing practically the same circuit, every town he came to, Silas had just been there.

Johnny Q thanked the clerk and headed to the men's room to open up the CDs he'd purchased and read the liner notes. As he sat down, he was distracted by a copy of *Tobacco Scene*, the area's free arts weekly, which was neatly folded on top of the toilet paper dispenser. He quickly turned to the music section to see if anyone previewed him—doubtful, since he hadn't gotten any calls for interviews. When he got there, the centerpiece was filled with a full-page article on Silas Henderson, complete with a photo of the man looking appropriately rugged with cowboy hat and 5 o'clock shadow. Johnny Q didn't read it; he turned the page and happened upon a small three paragraph review of *his* new CD, four stars, which took about two seconds to get through, as the writer mainly regurgitated the promotional sheet his publicist had crafted. But he added an original thought or two at the end and then plugged Johnny Q's gig, although the starting time was wrong, late by half an hour. On the opposite page, there was a half-page advertisement for Silas Henderson's new CD, *Dusty Roads and Roaring Engines*. Disgusted, Johnny Q finished his business and headed back to the café where he ordered an ice latte and surveyed the crowd he'd be playing to for the afternoon's second set.

Normally, at this point, Johnny Q would've gone around the tables, talked to folks, said hello, maybe moved some product. But, he just wasn't up for it. He still had a couple minutes, so he walked over to the stage area to fiddle with

his guitar and pretend like he was doing something. Three college students closest to the mike stand were engrossed in some sort of passionate conversation, but as he passed, one of them, a girl with shy eyes and full lips, stopped him.
"Do you have a minute?" she asked.
"Sure," he answered.
"I love that last song you played, I heard it on NPR, that's why I came, well, why we came," she laughed, nervously he thought.
"Really?" he said.
"My name is Joy," she said, holding out her hand.
He wrapped his fingers around her rather clammy hand and shook. Johnny Q sat down, figuring he could push his break a little, as there weren't that many people in the house.
"I'm Brendan," the boy across the table shot out.
"Alisa," the girl next to him said.
They shook hands all around, but Brendan went back to talking to Alisa and Johnny Q continued his conversation with Joy.
"Are you going to be playing some more?" Joy asked, gesturing to the P.A., which was buzzing louder in his absence.
"Yes."
"Oh good, because we only got here for that last song."
Johnny Q wondered how he could've missed her. Joy smiled constantly, but there wasn't anything phony about it, she just seemed like the kind of person who would smile even when she was angry. It made the light dance off her nose ring, he thought.
"I love your style, your melodies are so distinct." Joy added, "They really pull me in."
Johnny Q thanked her, raising his voice a little to be heard over the P.A., which was now buzzing even louder. Startled, she dropped the plastic lid of her latte and bent over to pick it up. The top couple buttons of her shirt were open and she took her time straightening up. Johnny Q suddenly felt better about the gig. Like a drowning man at sea, he'd been thrown a life preserver. And so he scrapped his idea of trying out new material in the second set, deciding instead to concentrate on "chestnuts" from the past, as he tried to hook at least one new set of eyes and ears.

After the set, Johnny Q talked to Joy for what seemed like a long time. She wanted to know where he was off to next, and he told her and she thought out loud how exciting it must be to live life on the road. She jokingly asked if she could roadie for him. She also told him a lot about herself, but that was common to his experience, people tend to open up to performers, even at his level. But, unlike most people he met on the road, the more she talked, the more he liked her and wanted to get to know her better. She didn't fit any particular category, and as Johnny Q sipped his fourth iced latte of the afternoon, he learned she came from a large family, had two sisters, was in graduate school getting her master's in social work, and after that, she wanted to do something with at-risk youth. She talked about how getting a good start in life was essential, and how so many kids didn't have the advantages she'd had growing up.

"It's not a fair playing field," she said.

Johnny Q felt something inside. Now, he wanted to marry her.

"Can I buy a CD?"

Johnny Q thought about this. If he gave her one, he might get started on a path that would never end, and the next thing he knew he'd be an at-risk performer. So he compromised and cut her a deal. She asked him to sign it. He wrote something short and sweet and scrawled his name with a sharpie pen he'd brought along for just such an occasion. The bookstore was growing quieter and Johnny Q heard Silas Henderson's affected Massachusetts-born country twang wafting in from the CD section. Joy's friends were starting to show signs of impatience and restlessness as they cleaned off the table and returned their rental books and magazines. Johnny Q saw his opportunity slipping away and so he stumbled forth, asking her out to dinner. She demurely thanked him and said she'd love to, but Alisa was the driver and they had to get going because her cousin was visiting from out of town and would be arriving soon and they'd promised to meet her and it was quite far away and they were probably late already. Johnny Q wondered how far anything could be from anywhere in Greensboro and Winston-Salem.

"Can I sign up on the mailing list?" she added, abruptly. "I'd love to see you next time you come to Greensboro to play."

Johnny Q figured that might be never. But, he played it cool, handing her his clipboard as he leaned back to watch, one hand on the back of the chair she sat in as she leaned in and wrote down her information. He thanked her and she offered her hand for him to shake, which he did, warmly. Then he watched her get up and walk past the empty tables and barren magazine racks, through the discount section, out the doors and into the twilight. He packed up, got paid, and did his totals: a hundred bucks to get him to the next place, a CD for the road, a magazine, and thirty-five bucks in CD sales. Oh, and he had an e-mail address and smiley face on the mailing list from a girl he'd like to marry. Maybe it hadn't been so bad after all. Like his manager said, it would be the six times in-between that would kill him.

The Town Crier

I live on the corner of East 2nd and Avenue B, across the street from an abandoned brownstone. A bunch of squatters used to camp out there, until the cops moved in and set up shop right on the street, in one of those mobile homes you always see at construction sites, wooden handicapped ramps leading them in and out like donuts on a conveyer belt. The red light is on, so to speak, a 24-hour watch to protect somebody's property, which makes me wonder exactly who owns that building. There are side benefits, however, like the fact that I never have to lock my car anymore. In New York City—can you believe it? What a trip . . . .

Anyway, it's a funky neighborhood and pretty quiet most of the time, except for the occasional Puerto Rican hotrod zooming down the block blaring salsa music out of two monster 20-inch speakers mounted in place of the back seat, woofers pounding away in orgasmic motion if you could see through the smoked glass windows. Oh, and there's this old guy who sits on the steps of that abandoned building, shouting an endless string of babble to the passerbys. Day in and day out he spouts a geyser of information, everything from current events to historical dissertations, waving his crooked fingers in accompaniment, as he conducts the movements of the street. He starts about nine in the morning and doesn't stop until after five, and you gotta hand it to the guy, I don't even think he breaks for lunch. I know, because I work out of my home and this has been one hot summer, so my windows are always open. In fact the wooden frames are swollen and jammed in place, and along with a barely detectable breeze, his rap comes steadily streaming in. Sometimes I look out and see him working it hard, his pockmarked face raised to the sky waiting for The

Big Guy's thunderous applause, I guess. Everyone in the neighborhood calls him "the town crier."

This friend of mine who works at a record label lives upstairs and the last time we hung out, I suggested that he should tape the crier, lay a hip-hop groove behind it, and put it out. He'd have a number one on his hands. I gave the idea away, can you believe it? That's just the way I am. I don't know, he'll probably never use it. But, I heard it right away, and as the summer gets longer and hotter, it makes more sense. Ladies and gentlemen, the town crier, putting on a show, the town crier, baby here he goes.

> *I cry for Puerto Rico,*
> > *you know it should be a state*
> *I cry for politicians*
> > *and what they'll never say*
> *I cry for this nasty weather, you know,*
> > *it's fallout from the bomb*
> *I cry for Belafonte*
> > *and the day-oh-day-oh song*

Boom shucka boom, I can hear the heavy bottom riffing off a staccato drum line, carrying the words downtown, where beat boxes all over Tompkins Square will pick it up and lift it across the millennium. I see the town crier on their shoulders, their knees bent in a loose and jangly soul dance that'll circle the city like a gravitational force. Scratch that shit, it'll fly in L.A. too, and all parts in-between, because the so-called "disenfranchised" roll off the treble on their stereos and get the message.

> *I weep for the landlord*
> > *polishing his gold*
> *I weep for the baker*
> > *and his day old jelly rolls*
> *I shed tears for the victims,*
> > *the rights of the accused*
> *I shed tears for the women*
> > *and children being used*

Dylan used to rap. Chuck Berry, too. Drop the coin right into the slot, yougottahearsomethingthat'sreallyhot. Blues cats before that. Man, I don't know why so many of my middle-aged white compadres are so afraid of these words and this music. I guess they want to hold onto their "classic rock" forever, polishing their past until it shines brighter than it ever did before. You know what it reminds me of? It reminds me of the days when everyone's parents were digging on Pat Boone and Frankie Avalon, living in fear of the future and its messengers, wild men like Jerry Lee and Little Richard, who had their rap down and weren't afraid to use it. It makes me wanna holler. I'm on the fifteenth floor and it makes me want to take the stairs, one step at a time, stopping at each and every landing to knock on the door and climb inside and open up the windows. Wait! Stop everything, I hear some sisters in the background, some oohs and aahs laying down a bed of roses for the crier, and the old man bringing it home for the climax. He's got this bravado, see, but it ain't forced, and it ain't about bitches and dope—it's about knowing what's there to be known. It's like the Hudson, baby, it goes on forever, the rain to the river to the ocean.

> *I cry for St. Paul*
> *   and every sinner's death*
> *I cry for the Lord*
> *   and I talk to Malcolm X*
> *You can cry for what you want,*
> *   or you can face reality*
> *The Town Crier is my name,*
> *   sometimes they call me Crier D*

Okay, so I got carried away. I jacked things up a little, but for the most part, these are his words, he's got a million words and the scary thing is most of 'em make too much sense. Sometimes I think he's half-prophet, half-crazy person; other times, I think who isn't. It seems as if I've been sitting at this desk for two years straight, tapping on the keys, snacking on cold pizza from the night before, doubting and dancing and trying to make things happen, yet I've never made more dough than I have this summer. I owe it all to the crier, pushing the groove, standing between me and the ghost of laziness. The crier works it hard each and every day and I feel like I've got to keep up with him.

Sometimes I take a break and walk a couple blocks to the corner store to pick up an extra bag of bagels. I tell the clerk they're for the crier, and since he knows him, too, he usually throws in some free cream cheese. When I drop the bag off, the crier looks right past me, like I'm not even there, waving his arms, keeping everything in motion, constant, flux, the words, boss, the words. I did this maybe three weeks straight before I started thinking, I'd never seen the man eat, maybe he's just pitching the bagels. So, the next time I went through this routine, I spied on my man. I got home and went over to the window and saw a gray charcoal-splattered pigeon eating a bagel from his hand, a very cool sight to behold. The crier was holding one arm steady, thrashing with the other while he hollered out something about how Pete Rose should be in the Hall of Fame. The pigeon had one eye on the wildness, but stayed calm, popping up and snatching pieces of the bagel with its beak, probably cooing softly beneath the crier's steady rumble. I checked it out for awhile, and as the crier moved into a rant on the diamond cartel in Africa, a buddy joined the pigeon. Pretty soon, the bagel was gone and I went back to work. What a trip.

Anyway, I tapped away all summer, soaking in the crier and the cops, watching it all from my window when I wanted to and turning over lots of work when I didn't. Everything was smooth as could be, until one night when I fell asleep with the windows open, as usual, and was rudely awakened by the early morning sound of jackhammers ripping up the street and shaking the buildings with an earthquake-like intensity. I grabbed a robe and stuck my head outside to see what was going on. The cops' headquarters was intact but they were either huddled inside with their earmuffs on or out somewhere having breakfast. It was way too early, about 9 o'clock, and the skies were overcast and gray, which made the whole block look like it needed Prozac.

I could tell the day was gonna be a drag. Across the street, I spotted the crier doing his thing, but I couldn't hear a word. His arms were waving and his mouth was moving, but the construction was so loud, he probably couldn't even hear himself. From a distance, I saw that his face was all scrunched up, like he was in terrible pain, the personal kind, much worse than disgust over the sewer system or a Cuban blockade or whatever big issues he might have on his mind. It bummed me out. You know, when you stop to think about it, he's somebody's son, he's part of a family somewhere, and maybe he's even somebody's father. Who knows how he wound up here. I don't even know how I got here! It's like that Talking Heads' song, "this is not my beautiful home . . . how did I get here?" You know what I mean?

Anyway, it doesn't matter, the thing is this guy gave the neighborhood character and connected everybody in a weird way, like a corner deli or a newspaper stand, the man was dependable. Everybody knew him, we could talk about him or talk to him—he never answered back, but that was okay, we could always listen up.

Until now, all because of some annoying street repairs we didn't need in the first place. There were about a dozen construction workers circled around a big hole in the pavement, two had jackhammers in their hands, while the rest milled about and supervised. I guess the ten were there to make sure the other two made the hole bigger. Some kids on bicycles rode by, close to my building, and looked over their shoulders at the construction site as they passed. The crier was still out on the stoop, but his arms hung limply at his sides and his mouth was closed. His shoulders rippled back and forth like a pigeon ruffling its feathers, and I suddenly realized he was sobbing. The town crier was crying, I mean, it sounds funny, but it wasn't, it was a trip, and it broke me up. I couldn't take it anymore, so I pulled my shade and went into the kitchen to make a pot of coffee. The jackhammers kept hitting the street, splitting it into pieces and digging a bigger, deeper hole. The walls rattled, I was rattled, and when I opened the cupboard, I saw the coffee cups shaking like paper birds, beautiful and bent, never made to fly. That was a week ago and I haven't seen the man since, a hard time tapping, if you want to know the truth. The town crier, baby, listen to him cry.

Billy and the Tuba

From behind a tiny desk in a dusty office on the fifteenth floor of a massive structure set in stone on a city block built before his birth, Billy paid 25,000 claims. Dermatitis, vaginitis, gangrene, gout, rabies, scabies and cancer of the pancreas. Pulmonary arteries, cardiac arrest, ptosis, thrombosis, and abdominal pain—all those claims in a single year. With fingers like stogey stubs, he pounded the computer keys, doubled his production, hung a picture of his dog, and waited for his supervisor to bring the simple word of thanks that never came. 25,000 claims. In a single year. That's what Billy paid.

Billy's cubicle was a small dot at the wrong end of a very long kaleidoscope. Grotesque characters surrounded him, wandering back and forth across the office, criss-crossing in random. Out of the corner of his eye, he saw the fat lady, the bearded lady, the contortionist, and the midget. The carnival barker beckoned from deep inside the president's tent. Everything was covered with bright polyester poster paint. He could even smell the elephants. The only thing missing was the fun house.

Billy stared at his watch and felt the window behind him. It was too cold to go outside, even for lunch. Yankee winters made him sad and homesick, longing for the old days, when his mother was still alive.

Daddy used to play fiddle and rubboard in a bunch of bluegrass outfits around Kentucky, including a stint with Bill Monroe and his boys. He wasn't home much, always out on the road to somewhere, and one day he finally left the family for good. He wrote Billy a note he wasn't old enough to read. Mama did the honors.

Dear Billy; you're named after Mr. Monroe, so make me proud and learn to play this damn thing. Love, Daddy.

Well, it wasn't a fiddle and it wasn't a rubboard. And it wasn't a guitar or even a stand-up bass. The note was stuck to a huge white tuba. And the tuba stuck to Billy. Mama laughed in a funny way, like it was some kind of joke. Billy took it seriously, though, and grew up blowing that tuba day and night, sometimes until his lips bled. Pictures of John Philip Sousa hung on his bedroom wall. Time went on and Billy came to learn that his daddy won the tuba in a card game, from some fella in a big-top band. From that point on, Billy wanted to join the circus, so he too could play in a big-top band.

When the circus came to Louisville, Mama would make sandwiches and pack them into a single straw picnic basket. She'd wear her starched white dress, oblivious to the rust-spotted station wagon in which they rode. Billy blew tuba as she drove, puffing his cheeks up like a pair of hot-air balloons. They drifted over the cows a-grazing and the horses swishing their tails in the breeze. He could smell the manure. He could hear his Mama singing.

"Billlleeee!!!!"

"Yes, ma'am."

"Here's some more work for you. And I expect this done today. Before you leave!!"

Miss Debris dropped a thick brick of data onto Billy's desk and it landed with a hollow thud. She was a loud, abrasive woman, with fat ankles and plaid hair. She was meaner than a gander and a lot less protective. She was Billy's supervisor.

Billy despised the sound of Miss Debris's voice. Mama used to tell him it was okay to hate what a person's doing, but you shouldn't hate the person, because sometimes they just don't know any better. Still, Billy dreamed of turning the tables. A warm breeze swept down from the vent above Billy's head, blowing open a trunkload of memories. He saw a big old paddleboat down at the landing, water lapping at the shore. He saw a little boy with one leg on the landing, one leg on the boat. That boy better make up his mind soon, thought Billy.

Billy's dream gave him a large mahogany desk, plush carpeting, and a corner office with a beautiful view of the Ohio River. He sat behind the desk, wearing a top hat on his head, holding a bullwhip in his hand. The chair was elevated, making it easier for him to look down on his employees. He reached into a desk drawer and pulled out a big brown tuba, shoving it into Miss Debris' small stubby hands.

"Miss Debris, from now on you must practice this tuba five days a week, from nine to five each day. You may take half an hour for lunch. If at the end of each week, you have not met our production requirements, you will be expected to work overtime until you do so."

"But, Mr. Billy, sir, I have no need for the tuba. I'm terrible at it, and I don't even like music, sir."

Billy let out a crazy laugh in his dream, sneering as Miss Debris shrank into a cowering ball.

"That's beside the point, Miss Debris. You were hired to play tuba for us. Do you really think you can earn a living working on computers? Fat chance! Pick up that tuba and start practicing if you want to make something of yourself. Lord knows you'll never marry!!!"

Billy swung his bullwhip in the air and cracked it on the desk. Miss Debris fled from his office in a fearful fit, the big chocolate tuba rocking back and forth on her hulking frame. Tears rolled down her cheeks. Sweat slid down her ankles.

"Billlleee!!!!"

The smile dropped off Billy's face. He turned to meet Miss Debris' whiskered chin head-on.

"Yes, ma'am, " he answered weakly.

"Here's a file I forgot."

Another slab of data fell with another hollow thud, even deader than the one before. It sounded familiar to Billy, but for a different reason. He picked up the file and let it drop again, repeated the process, and began to place the sound. A horse pounded a hoof on a hard bed of sawdust, as the trainer snapped his fingers and waved his whip. Each of his questions was met with a dutiful reply and all the while the horse kept both eyes fixed on his master's hand. The big-top was bustling and the president was happy. The payroll clerk came by with his lump of sugar and Billy was home again.

Mama used to tell him that quitters never win and winners never quit. Furthermore, she said, "Quittin' is a cowardly thing to do, Billy; it's like suicide or somethin'. God don't take kindly to that." Those were her exact words. Billy would never forget them. He would never forget anything about his mother.

Billy struck a match off the bottom of his shoe, bringing the flame slowly to his face. He held the match still and watched the flame flicker and glow, rise and fall. It had a rhythm all its own, like an old-time carnival tune. He reached for a cigarette, but the match slipped from his fingers and fell into the cuff of a trouser leg. Mesmerized, Billy watched as his pants began to smolder. A long minute went by before he doused them with leftover coffee from his "Thank God, it's Friday" workplace mug.

Billy performed these actions as if he were repeating a sacred ritual, relearning habits long since forgotten. Then, he ripped open a file and spread its contents all about his desk. He ripped open another file. And another. Until there was a week's worth of work piled up on the center of his desk. He rolled up his shirtsleeves and dove in with both hands, kneading the small stack until he found a bill for first-degree burns. He giggled as he held it high, striking a match and lighting the edge of the claim. Again, he was mesmerized, watching the fire catch and gain momentum before he dropped it onto his desk at the last possible second. His laughter grew with the flames, slowly and steadily, up to the ceiling and out the door, riding high on a magic carpet of smoke. Miss Debris caught wind of the smoke and the heat and the laughter and came galloping down the hall. Billy's desk was ablaze by then, a calliope of fire syncopated by smoke alarms going off in perfect time, Billy's crazy laughter punctuating the mad symphony. Miss Debris' thunderous footsteps cued the crescendo and as she turned the corner, Billy leapt onto his desk, rolling back and forth in the flames, a conductor deferring to his score. The last thing he heard was a single tuba note, low and mournful. The last thing he saw was his Mama, holding her sides in silent laughter. They laughed together. She laughed last.

Kudzu

It surprises people when I tell them I used to sell kudzu. They only know me as a saxophone player, the old guy in the back with dark glasses who snaps his fingers and steps forth to blast a solo now and again, although most of the time I choose to underline the melody with a much smoother counterpoint. But, it's all true, and sometimes after a gig, if I've had a couple to drink, I'll take off the glasses and tell a lady I fancy that I've lived several lives, and in one of them, I used to sell kudzu.

It was back in Natchez, Mississippi, years ago, you could find me sitting on a small folding chair on the corner of the two busiest streets in the historic district, selling long strips of the vine, which were bound and tied with red and white ribbons. I'd tell the tourists who stopped to chat, cameras dangling from their necks like evolutionary appendages, that the natives were aware of the kudzu vine's many uses, including its magical healing properties. There was nothing magical about my position, as I repeated my rap fifty times a day, and they never knew that "native" referred to people like me. From where I sat, I could see the blazing sun and the cold moon rise over the banks of the Mississippi each and every day, and to hear some of those pocketbook strangers talk about the place, I should've been on my knees giving thanks.

But, I wasn't.

Most of the time I was restless and unhappy, like I had been returned to prison after a long escape, redeposited in a stagnant town spilling over with the kind of intense historical charm that could wear a man like me down. Behind the façade, it was people living their lives, just like anywhere, some good, some bad, most somewhere in the middle, well-meaning but too anesthetized to get a rise out of anybody. I was born there, but it was my father's town, really, and his father before that, one of those turn of the century renegades you read about in books, a regular law bending Horatio Alger, the kind of man who came to America with big eyes and a huge appetite and took what was there for the taking. My grandfather sailed into Natchez on a riverboat barge, landed under the hill, and to the surprise of everyone, including himself, he fell to the charms of a local girl.

He took some of his new money and bought a big piece of land in the respectable part of that old-money town, where he built a gleaming white mansion for my grandmother, something for her to look after when he was out doing whatever it was he did. The front of the house was framed with two huge white columns, his and hers, reaching from the ground to the top of the widow's walk. He added a big coach house out back for the servants and, later, a man-made pond, with a footbridge, so she could go out and fish for trout whenever she liked. They had one son, my father, who inherited the house and stayed in the thieving business and became a U.S. Senator, building roads and sewers and skimming cash, taking a little under the table whenever he could, back in the forties and fifties, in the days after Huey Long insisted every man was king, and before Martin Luther King was anything but a premonition.

I never felt comfortable in the house; it was too big for me. Who really needs that many rooms to have a good time? I didn't tell my father this, because I loved him as much as he loved the house. He was a good man. At first, we didn't see eye to eye on the saxophone, but I kept doing what I did and eventually he got used to it. When he lost his final campaign and retired, he had more time on his hands, so he'd come down and see me whenever we played New Orleans.

Now, at the time my father passed, my girlfriend Samantha and I were living together, in a little place in Brooklyn—Park Slope, which is where she's from. She is a very solid woman, unwavering, yet beautiful; easy to get along with, but if you cross her, ice cold. I suppose that's why we connected, she was everything I wasn't and vice-versa. I was out on the road a lot, and while people think this wears on a relationship, it was perfect for us. Whenever I came back from a tour, I took a week off, and we had another honeymoon. It was easy to live a life that was a series of honeymoons. But, despite it all, when father died,

I started thinking different. A death to someone close to you can make some people act funny, and do all sorts of things they wouldn't normally do. I suppose that's what happened to me, but it made me go sane, instead of crazy, though going sane, for me, was crazy, if that makes sense.

The whole point is I started to long for home and so I married Samantha and moved back to Mississippi, where we turned the big house I'd inherited into a bed and breakfast. It was time to settle down, maybe raise a family, I told myself. I did pretty good for the first six weeks or so. Then, I started getting itchy, I missed the music and the town got harder to take. Since I wasn't leaving and coming back, the sidewalks got narrower, the streets shorter, and the bars smaller. And the honeymoons were gone.

"You could always play with the bands down on the riverboat," Samantha would say.

"Yeah, right."

Once she mentioned that the band down at the Holiday Inn needed a horn player. People forget you know, it's a what-have-you-done-lately business, out of sight, out of mind. It was as if she'd forgotten all the highs, the Vanguard where we met, the tours that took us to London and Montreal and Paris; the gigs at Lincoln Center and Montreaux. Sure, I was always a sideman, but I'd had some good highs, back in the day.

Samantha took to the hospitality business, as they call it, with a firm and steady hand. Some of the wilder women I'd met before her were like that old ride on Coney Island, the one that occasionally malfunctions and throws an unsuspecting teenager to a tragic death or maiming every few years. But, Samantha, as I said, was very solid, and turned into a rock when she started working that front desk and pretty much organizing everything that needed to be done to keep our bed and breakfast running. I, on the other hand, with no identifiable skills to my name other than blowing scales on my horn, roamed from task to task like a handyman who wasn't really handy.

One of my regular contributions, however, was trimming the kudzu vines that grew everywhere on our little plot of land, up to a foot a day in summertime. It clung to trees, snaked across the yard, wound its way across the porch and scaled the walls. It was the plant world equivalent of the cockroach or Miles Davis, it kept coming at you in different ways, no matter what you did. Then, I got the idea that I should cut it down, but gracefully, each strand cut and tied into bundles to sell during tourist season. You'd be surprised what people will buy, and sure enough, in the months to follow, I sold more strands of kudzu than I ever did copies of my one and only *Midnight Moods* instrumental saxophone solo record. I didn't keep track, but I bet my kudzu bundles went gold.

This gig turned into quite a cash cow, because like the kudzu, tourists never stopped coming, flocking in droves, wearing colored t-shirts, khaki shorts and those loud plastic fanny packs, searching desperately for memories and, instead of building their own visions, identifying with purchase power, snatching up trinkets to be wrapped in tissue paper, taken home, and put on the mantel. I imagined some folks clinging to their objects forever, while others would let go in a matter of days, but it didn't matter to me what they did with their money as long as they spent some of it on my corner.

I'd never even owned a clock radio before the kudzu, but there I was, setting the alarm early and sneaking into the kitchen to pack a survival kit, a flask full of rum and Coke, which I'd slip into my backpack before Sam realized I was up and about. As she was so solid, she wouldn't have understood that my survival kit was all I had to keep my thoughts from turning dark while I sat in the bright sun, thoughts that lost themselves in each other like the tourists ambling from one antebellum home to another. Sometimes, I'd just about lose it, and so, I'd slap a WILL BE BACK sign on the back of my chair and get up to walk around, wandering down to the riverbank to stare at the barges that lumbered downstream toward Baton Rouge, huge steel monstrosities, mechanical beasts of burden carrying a lot less charm than the majestic boats that brought my grandfather and others like him ashore so many years before. For me, the river was most beautiful when it was empty and free, powerfully changing on its own accord and the sight of those barges would only make me feel worse, like I was looking at a landfill in the middle of the Grand Canyon. My grandfather probably would've laughed, poured himself a long one and toasted the world of percentages and progress. But, me, I'd take another pull and feel sorry for myself, knowing I was weeping for more than the river.

This was my routine, it flowed unchanging from moment to moment, hour to hour, until one day something happened to flood the banks. I was manning my corner, sipping away and pulling the brim down low on my baseball hat to hide my face from the sun. The heat was oppressive and as I stood up to unstick the hot vinyl chair from my butt, a tall man wearing a buzz cut and a shoulder bag approached from across the street. He took large deliberate steps and reached me quickly, stuffing a fifty-dollar bill into my hand and buying me out. He told me that every seven years one's life changes, it was Zen philosophy, he said, if you let go of desire, you will have visions that lead you to truth. He stood still for a moment and then abruptly turned on the pivot, walking westward toward the river, weighted by the vine.

I wasn't into religious bullshit, it didn't matter to me if you were Christian, Moslem, or Buddhist, if you put it into words, you were full of dogma, trade one crutch for another and you're still crippled, is what I thought. But, since I was suddenly without kudzu, I was just happy to be able to head home. I got in the car and put Coltrane on, no words, no dogma, just sounds that make you realize that great things still happen in the world all the time and sometimes you get to see, hear, or touch them.

I took the same route home I always did, Franklin to Martin Luther King Drive, turning onto John Quinlan Road, which led directly to our bed and breakfast. I turned again past the second gate, into the long gravel drive that led to our home, the two commanding pillars on either side of the front porch beckoning me through the trees. The house had been painted recently and its whiteness was blinding, in contrast to the dark and wild foliage that covered our sprawling yard. I parked the car at the end of the drive and walked toward the office, which was also the rear entrance to the house. I lit up a cigarette, to cover the smell of liquor on my breath and avoid a lengthy inquisition from my detail-oriented wife, who I can tell you, was very very solid.

"Samantha," I shouted as I entered, feeling black and white and not unlike I was lost in some old television show, only I was the square 9-to-5 man who marries a sexy witch and then won't let her use her powers. Can you imagine such a thing? Shit, I'd be flying all over the world on her magical credit card, figuring out how many different places we could make love, rather than trying to dream up another stupid ad hawking diapers or toilet paper to the disappointment of my cranky boss. Anyway, I called for my Samantha, but all I heard was the endless creak of an old house. Then I noticed that there was a note for me, taped to the phone by the front desk. She said she'd gone out to do some grocery shopping and would I trim the vines outside the second floor windows while she was gone.

I *hated* trimming those motherfucking kudzu vines,

let me tell you, it was an endless task, and only pulled me deeper into that endless cycle of trim and sell, trim and sell. As long as I was trimming, I'd have to keep selling. But, I told myself it had to be done, this was my new life, and even if I was different than that Darren dude, no one was going to twitch her cute little nose and make my problems disappear.

And so I went to the shed out back and got the step-ladder and a long, sharp knife. The sun was still burning brightly, beginning of its long descent toward the horizon line. I set up the ladder against the house and climbed the wooden steps slowly, because I didn't much like heights. By the time I was level with the second floor, the back of my shirt was completely soaked with sweat, and I felt trails of disappointment running down the back of my calves. I put a hand on the side of the house to steady myself and started chopping, stabbing and cutting at those damn kudzu vines in a cathartic frenzy. I cut them with the sweeping motion of a blind man, stripping them from the house with which I'd been saddled, cutting and binding their oppressive, stran-gling limbs, taking them to my corner, close to the river where the water flowed endlessly and the lumbering barges carried their tonnage and I sold my time and soul to the steady stream of visitors who came and went and simply had no idea where I'd been or what I'd done. I attacked the kudzu vigorously, and as I did, I pictured those little bundles I carried each morning, seeing myself as one single strand within, strapped in place, unable to move. Chop and cut, I swung viciously and the breaking of the kudzu, loud and deafening to my ears, made all other sounds faint and dis-tant by comparison.

The ladder beneath my feet began to shake and soon I was tipping, dropping the knife, following it with my eyes as it fell to the grass below. Watching its flight made me nauseous and shaky and so I grabbed at the last remaining cluster of vines and held them strong as the ladder tipped away completely and crashed to the ground, leaving me swinging in mid-air, back and forth like Harold Lloyd in an old slapstick movie. I came to rest against the outside of the second story window, no guests were in the room at the time, unfortunately, or it would've been open and I could've climbed in. Instead, I had an out of body experience, no I didn't die, I just floated away from myself and stood back laughing, saying you sorry motherfucker, why don't you get back to what you were born to do?

And, after that, what I did was simple.

I let go.

A lifetime passed on that fall to the ground and when I hit, I jumped up and found myself unharmed. Towards the house I went, limping, walking, and then running. Upstairs in our bedroom, I hurriedly filled a suitcase with some of my old stage shirts, underwear, and a tattered copy of *Hot Water Music,* to read myself to sleep at night. I took some cash from the top drawer of the dresser and remembered that Miles and Coltrane were already in the car. I stopped cold for a long minute and surveyed the room, pulling on my memory and trying to put my finger on the something I'd overlooked. And, then, my eyes fell on the dusty black saxophone case languishing in the corner, nearly hidden behind an old wicker clothes basket. How low I'd sunk, I thought, to almost forget the reason I was leaving. I laid the case out on the bed, opened the latches and looked inside. She was still there, waiting; a little neglected and in need of some polishing, but like me, still in one piece. I shut the case quickly, and with both hands full, hurried to my car. I drove and drove, until I put enough distance between here and there.

At this point, the lady I fancy often asks me why I didn't leave a note for my wife. I suppose they think it was cruel or cowardly that I split the way I did. But, when this happens, I look the lady I fancy in the eye, as the lights go up and the bartender gets ready to send us out into the night to find each other, and say, "My dear, I didn't leave a note because unlike those tourists, a real lady is not the type to buy any old thing."

Somehow, this always works; it's the only part of the story they really believe.

Next of Kin

"Shiiit."

Mr. Leroy guzzled a beer, wiped his brow with the can, and slammed it down hard on the kitchen table.

"Shiiit . . . the cops'll take care of that shit. I don't know what the hell you're doin'. Shiiit."

He was straight out of the swamps, a coon-ass with kin still hidden in the tall weeds and murky water. Alligator bait. Deanne heard him say more to me in fifteen minutes than in all the years she'd known him. The heat was stifling in that kitchen.

"Man, why don't you just watch People's Court or somethin', 'stead of botherin' folks all over town. That's what cops are for. Shiiit."

Mr. Leroy smiled a half-toothless smile and gestured with his weatherbeaten hand. His comments were directed at his wife, Miss Carrie, and Deanne's grandmother, Miss Phyllis. An old friend of Carrie's had up and died the day before and they were taking it upon themselves to locate the next of kin—in this case, the younger sister.

"Shiiit, I just caulked the windshield on her car. Didn't get paid neither. Now she's dead. Shit. If you get a hold of her kin, tell her I want my twenty bucks."

He nudged me and cackled like we were sharing an old private joke. Deanne and I had only been together a short while, but I noticed from the start that she had an intense jealous streak. Experiences that belonged to her could be shared only when the time was right; otherwise, this encroached on her territory. I couldn't help it if Mr. Leroy took to me. But, that didn't matter. He took another swig of his beer and tugged on the bill of his New Orleans Saints cap. Sweat oozed through the mesh. Mr. Leroy didn't mind. Miss Carrie held a stubby index finger to her fat lips, stifling his laughter.

"Hello, I'm Missus Carrie Fontenot and I'm callin' about a Miss Mary Neville. She's dead. That's right. I'm a friend of hers and we're lookin' for her sister. Mary was found stone cold in her trailer, all by her lonesome. Been that way for at least twenty-four hours. Rigor mortis had set in and they said that . . . hello . . . hello?"

Miss Carrie bowed and shook her head emphatically, her greasy black hair flailing about like a dancer on a Mardi Gras float. She was a huge woman, reminiscent of a stack of tires, different sizes, all piled on top of one another. She played Hardy to Mr. Leroy's Laurel, beating the shiit out of him whenever he came home drunk. She had a gold-framed picture of Elvis on her television set and kept her Christmas lights up year-round.

"Can you top that? That woman hung up on me!"

"Carrie, people ain't what they used to be."

Miss Phyllis' words carried a certain authority, cocked and fired with the skill of a backwoods Zen master. It either came naturally or she was overloaded on Andy Griffith reruns, but either way, she considered herself quite the philosopher. She was a lot like Miss Carrie, only much thinner and of better breeding. I wanted to change the subject.

"Uh, excuse me," I said, treading lightly, "but if her sister is married, how do we know her name is Neville?"

Miss Carrie answered slowly, as if it was silly of me to ask.

"You see, when my friend Miss Nancy called, she told me that Mary's sister left her husband for another man." She paused. "This was 'bout two years back. Supposebly they livin' 'cross the river now, not far from Deanne's daddy."

Mr. Leroy grinned and got up for another beer. On the way back from the fridge he leaned down between Deanne and me and whispered in our ears.

"Shiiit, man, that's just old people talkin'. Gossip and shit. You know how old people are. Heh. Heh. Heh."

He was older than either one of them, but didn't give it a moment's thought. I liked Mr. Leroy. Nothing seemed to bother him. He and Miss Carrie used to live down the block from each other, in the old neighborhood, back on Magazine Street. Before the colored people moved in and ruined everything. Or so said Miss Phyllis. Mr. Leroy told me otherwise; he said the old neighborhood looked better than ever, but they just couldn't afford it anymore. Old Leroy was a coon-ass, you know. That's what everybody said. Seems people in New Orleans excuse all kinds of thoughts and behavior coming from a coon-ass.

Deanne started fidgeting and her expression grew tight and I could look behind her eyes and see the gears getting all wound-up tight. But, this was her nature. She hated anything that took attention away from her.

"If you know her sister ran off with another man, how do you know she's still a Neville?" Deanne pointed out. "She could've married the guy and changed her name. Or kept her first husband's name."

Miss Phyllis slowly lifted her eyes and peered over her bifocals and stared at Deanne as if she was from another planet.

"People do not do that. No woman wants her old husband's name hangin' around her neck."

"People do things like that all the time," Deanne insisted. "Henry and I knew a couple that decided they wanted to . . ."

"Honey, maybe up in Minneapolis they do that, but not here in N'Awlins," Miss Phyllis replied deliberately. "Things are different where you folks live."

"People are people, Grandma. I don't see why you have to be so stubborn about everything, I . . ." Deanne said, her words trailing off, sinking, left unheard by all except me.

Miss Phyllis's speech accelerated like the St. Charles streetcar run amuck. Their exchange went on for some time. She was nearly head-to-head with her granddaughter when she abruptly pulled the cord, slammed on the brakes, and ended the conversation. She returned her attention to the phone book, crossing off name after name with a large purple crayon. There must have been three dozen Nevilles listed.

"Hmmm, let's see now . . . Lincoln Neville . . . three-four-six, whoa, never mind . . . that sounds like a niggah name."

Earlier in the week, Deanne had explained to me that her grandmother never got over using that word. Why should she? That's the way things were. Miss Phyllis' best friend was a neighbor woman, black, and they checked in on each other from time to time to make sure everything was all right. I heard Miss Phyllis tell Deanne, "She's a great friend, honey, and I'd put her up against any white woman, any day of the week." That's the way things are, I learned.

"Uh, excuse me, Miss Phyllis," I began politely, "but don't you think the police would have contacted her family by now? It's nearly five o'clock."

"Shiiit, that's right," Mr. Leroy chipped in, "those cops'd go back to the station and turn on one of them computers. Just sit on their butts and push some buttons. They'd find her sister, though. Hope they find my twenty bucks."

Miss Carrie told Mr. Leroy to shut up and Miss Phyllis told

me to drop the formalities and call her Grandma. She crossed off another name. It was so hot in that kitchen even the crayon began to sweat. I was wondering how long this was going to go on. Mr. Leroy had an inexhaustible supply of Dixie beer. I was hungry. He kept poking me, telling me stories, and chuckling under his breath.

"Hello, I'm Missus Carrie Fontenot and I'm callin' about a woman by the name of Mary Neville. Yes, I know you have the same name. See, we're tryin' to find the next of kin. Mary was found stone dead in her lonely ramshackle trailer this mornin'. Not a soul in sight. You know, she'd been laid out like that for seven days!! That's right, her body was all rotten and the police had to wear handkerchiefs over their faces. Yes, I'm sorry, well . . . thank you. Enjoy your dinner."

"Shiiit, she wasn't there no seven days."

By this time, Miss Phyllis had crossed out about half the Nevilles in the phone book. They called maybe two-thirds of those and eliminated the rest because they were niggah names. Once I suggested they call one of the Marys listed and ask for the name and number of her sister. Deanne did not like this remark because she did not think of it. She was ready to blow. Mr. Leroy nudged me one last time before he passed out.

"Shiiit, Henry, don't ever get married."

His head lay on the table, surrounded by a halo of empty beer cans.

Around six-thirty, Miss Phyllis finally closed the New Orleans phone book . . . and promptly reached for Gretna, the nearest suburb. She chose a blue crayon for this task. Deanne buried her head in her hands. I patted her on the back and told her not to worry, I was sure they'd find the missing sister.

"They'll never find her. Don't you understand?!?!"

Deanne leapt up in a rage, shaking the kitchen table so violently that some of Mr. Leroy's beer cans fell to the floor and nearly woke him up. She shouted something about going back to Grandma's house to listen to some Neville Brothers records. She slammed the back door behind her. Irv's Auto Parts calendar trembled in her wake, gradually swinging to a halt under the watchful eye of Miss Phyllis.

"Your sweetheart has a sick sense of humor, " she said, "but I give you credit for putting up with it. It's just like her stepdaddy, treatin' her like she was one of his own. Any man who marries and takes another man's child, that's a good man."

I wondered what choice he had. He was married to someone else at the time, banging Deanne's mom, and looking for an out. What else was he going to do? Mr. Leroy would have agreed with me, had he been conscious.

"Hello, I'm Missus Carrie Fontenot and I'm callin' about a certain Miss Mary Neville. She's dead. Found this mornin', all by her lonesome, in a ramshackle trailer in the poor part of town. The police said she had a heart attack and then cracked her skull on the bathroom floor. You know, she laid there, stone-dead, for fourteen days before they found her!!! One policeman threw up and the others had to wear gas masks, just to carry her rottin' body away. See, now we're tryin' to get a hold of her sister, the next of kin. You wouldn't happen to . . . yes . . . thank you."

The doorbell rang and I jumped up to answer. I thought it might be Deanne. I opened the door and saw a young woman of about twenty-five, comfortably standing on the porch and studying the brick work as if she knew it well. I thought she might be one of Deanne's old friends. She was quite stunning, with deep dark green eyes and flaming red hair that reminded me of a sunset. She looked a little tired, and when she saw me, she straightened out the wrinkles in her short black skirt. A fine pair of well-tanned legs stretched long and slow from the black to the ground. She was barefoot.

"Good evening. Is this Mr. Fontenot's residence?"

I told her that it was and that I was a friend of the family. I said he was napping and did not want to be disturbed, a half-truth, I suppose. I asked if I could help, in any way at all.

"Well, no, I was hoping that . . ."

She let her sentence dangle and hang in the hot and steamy summer air. She looked in the sky, on the sidewalk, in the bushes—everywhere but straight into my eyes. Finally, she reached out and handed me an envelope she must have been hiding behind her back.

"Well, I guess it's all right. This belongs to Mr. Fontenot, so would you please be kind enough as to see that he gets it? Don't give it to anyone else, just Mr. Fontenot."

I assured her I'd give it to no one else. She held out her hand and I shook it lightly, like I was fanning a bouquet of flowers. Then, she smiled and turned and walked back to her car. I watched her every step of the way; her hips, her legs, her ankles. People sure acted funny around here, I thought. When she drove off, I spotted a line of caulk along the edge of her rear windshield, and from where I stood it looked white enough to be fresh. I tore the envelope open. Inside I found a wildly scribbled note and a twenty-dollar bill. The stationery read "From the Desk of Nina Neville." Some of the ink was smeared, but I was able to get the gist of the story. It went something like this . . .

"Dearest Leroy. Thank you so much for fixing my sister's windshield. I'm enclosing twenty dollars for your troubles. I'm sorry I had to ask you to leave this morning, but I needed some time alone. Mary and I were very close and it will be difficult making the necessary arrangements. Thank you for offering your help, but I'm afraid Miss Carrie might let on, if we spend too much time together. The past two years have been wonderful and I don't want anything to change. Looking forward to next weekend. All of my love, Nina."

There were a bunch of Xs and Os after her name, as well as a bright red lip-print. My mouth dropped open. I stuffed the twenty-dollar bill in my pocket and re-read the note as I walked down the block to Miss Phyllis' house. Deanne was inside and the winds had changed, for she welcomed me with an over-sized hug. I spontaneously offered to take her out for gumbo, my treat.

"What happened? Did they find Mary's sister?"

"They sure didn't," I said. "I'll tell you about it at dinner."

On the way into the city, we had the windows open and the radio on, and the oldies station was playing an old obscure B-side by Irma Thomas. I thought of the old cliche that says a pretty girl is like a melody, and how words spoken frequently become cliches because at their essence, they hold a grain of truth. After all, you could go deeper and say all women are like melodies. Some are sugary and obvious and hit you right upside the head and don't let go, wearing thin like the worst kind of anthemic top 40 song. Then again, some make an impression through casual grace, sneaking up on you with sophistication and making a home in your subconscious, turning over and revealing themselves to you in different ways over the years, in ways you probably didn't even realize at first. Deanne stared out the window while I had these thoughts, smiling quietly.

In the Garden District, we parked the car underneath a broken streetlamp and walked past an old cemetery, tree limbs casting shadows on the sides of faded white tombs. We held hands, but remained quiet. I ate heartily that night, and although I'm not much of a drinker, I ordered a bottle of Dixie, just for Mr. Leroy. I knew which kind of melody Nina Neville was; as for Deanne, I still wasn't sure.

Stage Energy

It had been two days since she'd driven Old Blue, and in those two days, snow had fallen, melted, and froze again, casting waves of ice across the car. Cindy picked up a rock and chipped at what should have been a space behind the driver door, watching as pieces of dirty ice fell to the ground like casual friends. Hurriedly and persistently, she repeated the process several times. Then she tried to force her key into the keyhole. It was sealed shut. She got out her lighter and held it to the surface. Pearls of water formed and she quickly slipped her key inside and turned in one quick motion, hoping it wouldn't break off. Success came as she pulled the door open.

Once inside the belly of Old Blue she turned the defrost to high, cracked the window open and lit a cigarette. The wind was picking up, and the sky looked ominous, as if more flurries were on their way. She waited a few moments for the defrost to start kicking in and then dove back into the Chicago tundra to clear enough space to see through while she drove. She took off one of her boots and, standing on one foot, pummeled the windshield with the sharp heel to speed the process, jagged slabs breaking up and scattering. Pretty soon there was a small window on the window. It would have to do.

Traffic south on Ashland Avenue was unusually heavy for late morning. Her fingers were numb from the cold, her down coat was zipped tight and her wool hat was pulled over her ears. She tried not to breathe too much, lest it fog the window. "This sucks," she thought, "why didn't I move to L.A. when I had the chance?" She hadn't made it two blocks when the car hit a patch of ice, sliding off to the right, towards the curb. "Shit fuck" she hollered as she dropped her cigarette, grabbed the wheel and turned it in the direction of the skid, exactly as she'd been taught in driver's education class. The cigarette flared out on her wet jeans, and the car butted up against the curb, straightened, and came to a stop. Luckily, she hadn't hit anything. Luckily, it was a free parking space.

She looked at her watch. "Shit fuck" she shouted to the sky, words deadened by the cold air. She grabbed her purse and left the car in the space the universe had found for it. She walked the two blocks to the nearest el stop, bought a ticket for the Ravenswood and huddled under a heat lamp with twenty-five other freezing commuters. It didn't make things any warmer. It was going to be one of those days.

She'd only "spoken" with music journalist Ken Dunk by phone and e-mail, but she immediately recognized him by his tortoise-shell glasses and spiky black hair. He was sitting at a little round table by the window, drumming his fingers on the chessboard top, tapping his Chuck Taylor laden feet on the floor. They exchanged pleasantries. "I'm sorry I'm late," she said, counting twenty minutes on her watch.

Ken looked surprised. "No worries, I didn't even notice." He rummaged through his satchel and emerged with a microcassette recorder. "Shall we?"

He began with the usual stuff, where she was from, how she got started in music.

"I've been playing clubs for some years now," she said. "It's a common story, really; I was a young girl and I saw the Beatles on Ed Sullivan and everything changed, but the twist was, instead of choosing to be one of the screaming girls, I wanted to be the one on stage."

He interrupted with another question, as if he was short on time.

"No, it wasn't a gender thing, at all. I wouldn't call myself a feminist," she said, in reply to his seemingly obvious inquiry. "It was about being the one doing, instead of the one watching—that's what interested me."

As soon as the words left her mouth, she didn't like the sound of them. She knew all too well the things that could be done with cut and paste by a disinterested journalist or incompetent editor, and hoped they wouldn't choose that line. She was a feminist; it was just that, well, words have multiple meanings, and sometimes she wished she was a painter because of it. Words could become labels, or worse yet, self-defining slogans. She knew some of these women who called themselves feminists, but many of them had husbands who pulled home big salaries and/or who made all the important decisions in their lives for them, and ultimately a lot of that sisterhood shit was just plain phony. Then again, maybe she was just jealous, she thought, staring out the window at the people rushing through the dirty snow and slush on their way to work. "Why didn't I move to Austin while I had the chance," she mused.

Ken Dunk asked a more insightful question.

"I don't know, truthfully," she answered, adding the word she always used when she wanted to obscure the truth. "I thought I was savvy enough to have seen it all, but then again, some motivations are deeply hidden, in the same way some habits are hard to break. I guess the main catch with me has always been the music itself; once it gripped me, I couldn't let go."

And so she had ended their exchange on a rambling sentence that made no sense at all. Ken Dunk nodded and turned off the tape recorder. I really blew that one, she thought, if he uses that one, no one will know what the hell I'm about. It sounded rehearsed, too. But, just like a performance on stage, you couldn't take it back—it was all or nothing, it was always all or nothing. Some artists would've asked to see the copy before it ran, but she hadn't reached that level. If she had, she probably still would've let it go.

On the el, she picked a copy of the *Chicago Sun-Times* off an empty plastic seat and ran through the music listings. Some friends from Cincinnati were playing at Schuba's on Saturday; Roast Beef Ronnie and his band were over at Buddy Guy's, and Larry Jerkins and his vanilla songwriting were putting on a "special acoustic show" over at the Cubby Bear. Well, she knew one place she wouldn't be going that weekend. She turned the page and saw an interesting article about a new inner-city program for young girls called Girls In the Mix, which was designed to get at-risk teenage girls involved in music. The woman running the program said that participation in arts afford opportunity for teenage girls to fight isolation, develop new skills, explore interests, relax, develop self-confidence, make friendships, and replace self-destructive behavior with positive, life-affirming experiences.

"These positive alternative activities will help girls empower themselves and form their own voice," the woman said, "which is particularly important in countering a culture where silence or passivity is often encouraged among women." Cindy tore out the article and put it in her purse, thinking it could be song fodder. She wondered if she would've taken part in such a program, when she was young, if it had been available. She doubted it.

Off the el, and down the steps, she walked by Old Blue, still safe, sound, and frozen. Back at her place, she took a long cleansing shower. That night, she had a recording session, some new songs to cut, it was time to try and hustle a deal to replace the one she'd lost. She felt her momentum fading, so she dried herself off, put on the baggiest sweatshirt she could find and crawled into bed for a nap.

When Cindy awoke, she poured some French roast into a coffee press, fired up the stove, and turned on her computer. There were only three new e-mails awaiting her.

First one: *John Norris would like you to view John Norris' Space! Hey Cindy. I have been a fan of yours for quite some time. I have seen what you are up to lately and wanted to introduce myself. Explore my journey at your leisure. You and I are both songwriters with a soulful bent and seem to have much in common. Would love to hear your thoughts. John Norris*

She ran into John about a year ago, at Jewel, while shopping for beer and pasta. He had been so forthright in introducing himself, it freaked her out at first, as he told her that he was a big fan and he loved this one particular song of hers that he'd downloaded from the web. She remembered about how when she started playing music, when folks would tell her they liked her stuff, it was because of something they *bought*. "I'll check it out, John," she replied. He'd learn, she thought; if he kept at it, he'd learn.

Second e-mail was from an old friend: *Hey, Cindy, I was wondering when you were coming out to New York to play. It's been a year since I've been here, I can't believe I haven't done a show yet—I wish I was as good as you at promoting myself. Well, hope you're well. Susie and Chip.*

Cindy had heard versions of this one many times, as if the only reason she had a career was because she was good at promoting herself. If you don't get out and do something, of course nothing will happen, but of course there were a lot of insecure egomaniacs out there expecting the ghost of John Hammond to come knocking on their door. Besides that, Cindy couldn't decide which was more annoying—her friend's "MRS" license plates or the fact that she signed all her e-mails Susie and Chip. She decided it'd be better to answer this one later.

Third e-mail read: *Hey there, I was at the show in Minneapolis. I went to your website and got this email addie. You know, the show was great, but you were better. You have great stage energy.*

Cindy mulled that one over.

"Thanks so much," she tapped away, "it was a really fun night."

It hadn't been that fun to begin with, it had started out like one of those nights that made her wonder if she shouldn't have decided to do something else with her life. The sound man was sick, the club owner was on vacation, the room was in shambles, and when show time rolled around, it revealed an unusually weak turnout in what was a usually strong market for her. As she had played, she had struggled to connect with the audience. They were so still and quiet, she thought she wasn't getting through at all, and at times, she had difficulty concentrating. But, she per-severed, and after the show, she was flooded with CD sales, kind words, and a super fan who owned all of her CDs and had traveled 100 miles to the show, which all reminded her that her music existed for a reason beyond her personal struggles. In short, it wound up being one of those nights that made her glad she'd done exactly what she had done, so far, with her life.

Cindy cut and paste this last e-mail and put it in her running "nice comments" e-mail file that she kept for dark moments when she needed her confidence built. As she finished her coffee, however, Cindy couldn't help but won-der if sometimes people indeed liked her more than they liked her music.

Later that night, Cindy was driving the other direction up Ashland Avenue, pondering the night's session. She was excited about the material, and David was enjoyable to work with, a talented and easygoing engineer who certainly got the most out of his tiny basement studio. But there was another part of this that she dreaded. The rhythm section she'd hired were top-notch players who delivered expertise but not always soul; and, more importantly, she felt they didn't always take her seriously. In many ways, she'd ac-complished more through her records and publishing deals than they ever had, but somehow their egos were tied to their impenetrable self-appointed local hero status. Then again, maybe they just didn't like her tunes—or worse yet, maybe it was because she was a woman.

As she drove, she scribbled on a notepad she had stuck to the dashboard with one of those rubber suction cups. One word—masks. It would trigger her later, seems everyone wears masks, it doesn't matter how big or small you are. Any musician or artist you know about, they all just wear different masks to get there—the cute mask, the quiet mask, the arty mask, the jolly mask, the world-saving mask, the underground mask, the show-biz mask. She tore off the piece of paper and tucked it into her purse sitting on the seat beside her. It could make for good song fodder.

Cindy pulled up in front of David's three-story brick brownstone, stone steps leading to a wide porch, presently covered with pine cones and holly for the holiday season. She parked on the street and step-slid her way up the frozen walk. His German shepherd started barking the moment she set foot on the first step. When David opened the door and welcomed her, the dog happily jumped up and sniffed at her crotch, and she petted it firmly to move its head way. She heard chatter in the basement.

"They're here already?" she asked David, surprised.

"R.B. just got here. Eric and Fred were about twenty minutes early, they came together." He smiled sardonically. "And I had to entertain them."

"Poor you," she said, hugging him with her free arm.

She set down her guitar and he took her coat. Last time she worked with Eric and Fred, they were twenty minutes late, and though she didn't say anything, her icy stares had set a bad tone for the evening. She took off her gloves and held her hands over a radiator in the kitchen to warm them for playing. Downstairs, the men kept on talking, and she could pick out the voices.

Eric Batt, the bassist, was tall and a bit overweight, some called him "the Fridge;" he used to play in a well-known local bar band called Fuzzy Dice back in the day, a five-piece outfit who packed out clubs from Aurora to Lyons to Tinley Park with their easily imitated combination of recognizable covers and forgettable originals. Cindy was in a band that used to open for them once in awhile, back at the Thirsty Whale of all places, a disco ball dive bar in River Grove; it was so long ago that she wasn't even legal at the time. Every time she saw Eric, she remembered how cool Fuzzy Dice had thought they were, hair piled up high, skinny leather ties and bright red tennis shoes, and how no one in the band ever talked to her backstage. Well, the hair was gone, and so was the tie, and now Eric had become one of the more sought after players in town. He was a quick study, she had to admit, and got a good sound when he didn't rely on that faux funk string popping shit.

The drummer's name was Fred. He had a last name that started with D, but he insisted that no one use it, and over the years, he'd taken to painting Fredd on all his bass drums, not in large letters, but in block print on one quarter of the skin. He was more open than Eric, generally. He'd always been a bit of a gun for hire and Cindy guessed he'd learned flexibility and survival early. Fredd's main paying job was teaching drum lessons, and he also wrote for a drumming magazine on the side. He was always talking about the corporate gigs he was doing and seemed to equate every professional success with how much money he made. She couldn't imagine having conversations like that with John Lennon or Joni Mitchell or any of the people that made her pick up a guitar in the first place. Yeah, they wanted to be rich and famous, but somehow it was still the music first, and talking corporate wouldn't have been the mask they'd have chosen.

Finally, silent save for an occasional three-word sentence, was Roast Beef Ronnie, the guitar player. R.B., as they called him, had played in blues-based combos around the city for years, including a stint as Tyrone Davis' bandleader, which Cindy always found impressive. R.B. was a guy who missed the beat craze by about seven years, but never really gave up the ghost; you could see it in everything from his gravelly way of speaking to the soul patch he wore with pride. He favored long sleeves and sport coats no matter how hot it was outside, which caused many rumors around town. Cindy knew his playing and respected it immensely, but hadn't worked with him before this evening. He came in on David's connection.

As she stood at the landing, their voices grew louder, as Eric and Fredd laughed and went on about a gig they did the previous weekend backing up Larry Jerkins. Jerkins had been in about seven bands since she'd been on the scene, all equally boring and mainstream, yet somehow always well-liked in the local media, particularly XRT and other local radio stations who favored play lists that were lost in time. He was seemingly everywhere at all times, and she never understood how or why and whenever she heard praise for his supposed brilliance, the short hairs on her neck rose like prickly heat. "Why hadn't she moved to New York when she'd had the chance?" she wondered.

She felt David's presence behind her as she stood listening. Think positive, put it out of your mind, and visualize success, she repeated to herself again and again, bounding down the stairs and into the basement. The chatter stopped quickly, as if they'd been discussing a night at strip bar.

"How you guys doing?" she offered.

Fredd responded with a hearty "Killer, Cyn, just killer." Eric said nothing, as he pretended to fumble with his strap. R.B. had his back to her, dialing knobs on his amplifier, searching for a sound.

"All set up and ready to go," Fredd went on, with fake energy. "Check it out, I just got these new cymbals on an endorsement deal, this'll be the first time I use 'em, aren't they great? After this, I have a corporate gig on Saturday, and . . ."

Luckily, R.B.'s random dialing drowned out the rest of Fredd's sentence.

David got some levels and soon, they started in on the first of three songs they were to cut, an up-tempo soulful tune titled "You Burned my Bridges," which was semi-auto-biographical and written in broad strokes, in an attempt to try to pull a positive out of a negative. People liked positive, up-tempo, that's what her plugger used to say to her. It made her sick to think his words had sunk in and stayed with her, but then again, with a title like that no one was going to mistake her for Up With People.

She strummed a few bars for Fredd and he pulled out his handheld electronic metronome and asked her if that was the right tempo. Against her better judgment, she nod-ded yes, and the song kicked off and they ran through the take and it was indeed too fast. Fuck that plugger, she thought, I need to trust my instincts on this, and so she asked Fredd to slow it down. He did and they tried again, but the rest of them pushed the tempo, leaving it closer to where it was. She was already frustrated and they'd barely begun.

"Can it be like . . ." and she thumped out the beat on table with her hand. "Would it help if I sang a scratch vo-cal?"

"Sure," grunted Eric, "but it'd still be too slow."

"Let's just try it," she sighed. R.B. laid a nice soulful guitar line over the intro, but the song still wasn't clicking. They finished it anyway, and after the take, there was si-lence.

"What do you think David?" she asked, looking for sup-port.

He smiled. "Umm, well, I don't know . . . it depends on what you're going for."

Eric popped open a bottle of beer. The cap fell on the concrete floor and made a loud pinging sound which resonated in their silence.

"Nice guitar," David finally said, pointing to her telecaster.

"Thanks, you've . . ."

"Wanna sell it?" he added, deadpan, causing them both to laugh.

It never failed to break her up; once she'd hired a guitar slinger in town named Guitar Joe to do some lap steel overdubs, and all he wanted to do, the entire night, was buy up everyone's instrument. Later, they'd found he'd invented his own nickname. Who would nickname themselves anything, much less something as presumptuous as that? It would be like Songwriter Cindy or Engineer David.

Suddenly, R.B jumped in, getting them back on track. "I'm starting to feel it." It was the first thing he'd said all evening, and she was grateful, because he was probably the most respected musician in the house.

"Yeah," she added, "it's got to go at the slower tempo because I've got to be able to wrap myself around the words . . ."

She caught a barely audible snicker slipping out of Eric's mouth. Fredd tightened a wing nut on his cymbal. "It's up to you, Cyn, but I don't think the song works any slower. It's gonna drag," he added.

Cindy remained quiet, pondering which way to go. Pushing it might only further deteriorate the already tepid vibe they were laying down. Maybe she should just cut her losses and move to the next song. She was about to suggest this, when R.B. jumped in again.

"Man, let's just try it," he said, with a laid back drawl. "It is the lady's song. . . ." And then he laughed. "She is paying us 'cause we the best."

Hallelujah, thought Cindy.

"Ain't we?" R.B. added, loud enough for everyone in the basement to hear.

Eric and Fredd looked embarrassed.

"Shit, man, Tyrone woulda fined cats for less." No sooner than the words left R.B.'s mouth than Fredd started counting the song off with his corporate drumsticks. 1, 2, 3, roll, and they were in the groove.

The song turned into magic, exactly the tempo and feel she was looking for. There was a nice little soul backbeat, Eric was locked in with Fredd, and R.B. was doing his best minimalist bluesy guitar licks. It felt so good, they kept the song going quite a bit after the lyrics ended, after which they fell down around each other, musically, so to speak.

"That's a keeper," David shouted.

"Yeah, man," Fredd responded from behind the kit.

Cindy beamed and shot a glance at R.B., who was leaning his guitar against his amp.

"Take five, guys, I gotta run to the can," he said, heading for the stairs.

"I'm going up for a smoke," she added, to no one in particular, grabbing her purse as Fredd fidgeted with his cymbal some more and David showed Eric some new guitar he had just bought. Boys and their toys, she thought; aren't all guitars just pieces of wood with knobs on them? She hummed the melody of "Your Bridges Are Burned" as she ran up the stairs, two at a time.

When she hit the top, the bathroom door swung open and R.B. came out and they almost bumped into each other, doing a little mambo on the landing.

"Excuse me," he said, "but you are one talented songbird; that is one nice piece of work."

R.B. was so sincere, it made her heart stop. There was no bullshit, no angle, just one musician to another—and a musician she respected, to boot. She was about to thank him, when he added, "and you were right about the tempo all along. Don't let the fuckers get to you. They're only jealous." She must have looked surprised. "I mean it, because you are just too nice. Take it from R.B.," he added, patting her on the shoulder before running back down the stairs, all arms and legs and jumbled motion.

She went into the bathroom and sat down on the toilet. She was thinking about what R.B. had said, her mind racing ahead to the next two songs, what she was going to do with all of them once they were mixed, plotting, scheming, and dreaming, when she saw on the sink in front of her what must have been R.B.'s syringe, verifying the rumor mill.

Cindy had been around bands and clubs for years, but she'd never worked with a junkie—to her knowledge. She felt suddenly naïve. She stared at it for a moment and then touched the barrel, careful not to let her finger anywhere near the needle. She wondered how someone got there and where it took them, and although she'd always considered herself a risk-taker, the trip still felt foreign. She shook her shoulders, grabbed a tissue paper and wrapped up the syringe, and put it in her purse. She wasn't sure why—maybe she didn't want anyone to find it, maybe she was protecting him somehow, maybe she was, as he said, too nice. It wasn't even likely that R.B. cared; the man definitely seemed comfortable with his own skin. But, one thing was for certain, she thought, some people were too sensitive for this world.

It was warmer by the time she'd left David's, and when she got home, she noticed water dripping from an icicle on the front porch of her building. The radiator hissed loudly in the vestibule as she entered. She felt good, she had accomplished what she wanted, with her three latest and greatest songs demoed, backing complete, scratch vocals to be redone. There would be a minimum of overdubs. Inside, she lit up a cigarette, poured a glass of wine, and checked her computer. There were no messages, but it didn't bother her. It had turned out to be a pretty good day and she couldn't wait to get back to David's to finish the songs. There's no telling what they would lead to because at this point, she was positive it was her best work yet.

That's How Strong My Love Is

Roosevelt hunched over a battered upright piano, voicing chords with long slender fingers and humming softly under his breath. A fan blew hot air around the small, tidy apartment, barely cooling the place. He was used to that, it was always hot in Memphis. What he wasn't used to was finishing a song on this tight of a deadline. But, that's what Steve had told him; come on down Saturday and play it for us, Otis is looking for material. It was Thursday and he was almost done, but there was a logjam on the chorus. Lord, he needed a break. He experimented with a couple of chords, moving around the root and seeing what that did or didn't do to the chorus. Then he stopped and listened to nothing.

It was too quiet in the apartment, maybe that was it, he was so used to the sound of family, his wife and little boy moving about their four small rooms. They were visiting her mother in Jackson, and though he didn't feel quite right without them, it did give him time to write. Lord, he needed a break; his schedule was killing him, working in the blood bank all day, dim lights and repetition, and then writing into the night, sometimes just in his head, after the baby was asleep. Managing the Echoes was okay, but he really wanted O.V. and James to go secular, it was time, they could broaden their world and he could leave the hospital behind. He spun around on the stool and stood up, grabbing his shirt from where he'd dropped it on the coffee table.

Some considered pride the greatest of sins, but not Roosevelt, at least when he came to a shirt he could really be proud of. It had a tall-boy collar, hand-sewn stripes, and was completely made of cotton, so it hung cool and loose. His wife bought it for him down at Lansky's, and he thought of her as he put it on and walked into the bathroom to splash water on his face. He looked in the mirror. Man, he looked tired, there were dark circles forming on dark skin. Blood in my eyes for you, the old song goes. As he left the apartment, he stopped for a moment to glance at the empty bed and bassinet in the bedroom beyond the bath. Outside, he took a deep breath of night air and headed towards Beale, where he planned to take in some music and clear his head.

It was only a half-mile or so from where Roosevelt lived on Lauderdale to where he worked at Baptist Memorial, so he usually took the bus. But he drove on this particular Friday because he wanted to drop by a friend's house in south Memphis after work and go over some booking possibilities for his acts. So, after the day came to a close, he hopped in his car, rolled down the window, and took 240 south. After he took care of business, he drove the long way back north, on South Bellevue Road, passing Forest Hill and Calvary Cemeteries, all shadows and graves sequestered behind a rolling chain-link fence. He crossed himself even though he was Baptist, and didn't turn on the radio until he was well past their reach. He spun the dial a couple times with his index finger and heard nothing but the Beatles and the Rolling Stones, and some other English boys he'd never heard of. Roosevelt passed Elvis' house and wondered what "the King" thought about all them young bucks stealing his thunder. He chuckled to himself and turned to WDIA for about a block and then, still restless, switched the radio off and found the melody of his new song working its way back into his head. That was a good sign. He started singing the first two lines to himself, thinking of his wife.

> *If I was the sun way up there,*
> *I'd go with love most everywhere*

It was a strong beginning, no doubt; the song was becoming part of the world, meaning it now existed in a place beyond his vision. A good song did that, just like a child, it grows up and goes off on its own, and hopefully, becomes stronger over time. Roosevelt saw his songs as something of God, not self, little pieces of beauty that shone through an often darkened world. But he still wanted to make money off them, and he wasn't sure if this one was there yet. Maybe he had it, maybe he was just over thinking it, and maybe he was hungry and needed to work on a full stomach.

Roosevelt decided to pull into a Piggly Wiggly to get something to fix for dinner. As he circled the lot searching for an empty space, he ran across the strangest car he'd ever seen. It was a little snub-nosed thing, square as a box with a wide window in back, something like a cross between a golf cart and station wagon, and as he parked next to it, he noticed it was half the length of his Galaxy. He got out and walked around the car, surveying its small tires and complete lack of trim, and noticed two shadowy figures inside, one in the front seat, one in the back, each curled up in the fetal position. The window was fogged a little, so he knew they were breathing. No blood or shattered glass, either. How they could sleep all balled up in a car, in the Piggly Wiggly parking lot, he had no idea. They must be from out of town.

Roosevelt rapped on the window, driver's side. The parking lot lights were dim but gave him enough to make out a curly black head of hair slowly rising from the front seat. The figure opened his eyes sleepily and then, spotting Roosevelt, jumped back with a start, hitting his head on the steering wheel, cursing. He was a little younger than Roosevelt, pale skin and rumpled clothes, blue jeans and a sleeveless t-shirt with a picture of some guy playing an electric guitar and raising his fist in front of an American flag on it. Someone in the back began to move, and Roosevelt saw he was another white fellow, with dark freckles and straight red hair parted in the middle, long enough to grace the top of his shoulders. Roosevelt had only known jazz cats to wear their hair that long. After he got a better look, he thought that one might be an Army reserve, because his t-shirt proudly advertised the B-52s. Black curly hair started rolling his window down quickly.

"Hey, man, I'm not trying to rob you or anything," Roosevelt jumped in. He didn't want any Army rednecks going off on him just because he woke 'em to a bad mood. "I just want you to know it ain't too safe to sleep here."

Black curly hair's body language eased.

"Y'all been to Memphis before?"

"No, it's our first time," long red hair chirped in from the back. "My name is Don, this is Buck." He seemed completely at ease and this relaxed Roosevelt, in turn. No way was he an Army fellow, but they were definitely Yankees, he could tell from the accent.

"I'm Roosevelt," he said, reaching his hand inside to the fellow in the front. For some reason, their car didn't have a window in back, so he only waved at the other. "Listen, I tell you, I really wouldn't sleep here. But I have extra space at my place, my wife and kids are out of town, so uh

. . . if you want, you can follow me home, sleep on the floor for tonight."

The two boys looked at each other.

"You don't look dangerous to me," Roosevelt chuckled. "But, hey, if you don't, it's okay too, I just wouldn't sleep here."

"No, we'd appreciate it, it's very kind of you," Don shouted from the back.

"Sure enough," Roosevelt answered. "Sit tight, then, I'm gonna run into the grocery store for some food and I'll be back in a minute." He started to head in, and stopped. "What kind of car is that, anyway?"

"A Ford Escort," Don shouted again.

"Wild . . ."

Roosevelt drove slowly, keeping an eye on the rear-view mirror to make sure they didn't get lost or flattened in their little car. When he reached home, they followed him up the iron rail staircase that ran the height of the modest three-story brick apartment building. "It ain't much," Roosevelt said, as he pushed the door open with one hand and hung onto his bag of groceries with the other. "But it'll be more comfortable than your car." He pulled a six-pack out of the bag and put it in the refrigerator. "When these get cold, feel free. I don't drink, but I thought you might want something nice to cool you down," he said. "And I got some extra chicken, if you want something to eat. There's your sleeping area," he added, pointing to the living room. "Y'all can flip for the couch."

"Thanks so much," Don said, "this is really great."

"Yeah," said Buck, his first comment of the night.

"You're welcome." Roosevelt started tearing the cellophane off his packages of chicken. "Where you guys from anyway?"

"Chicago." Don pointed to the piano in the corner, and the guitar propped up next to it. "You play in a band?"

Roosevelt nodded. "Not really. But, I write a bit, and I manage some acts. Gospel groups, mainly. You play?"

"We're in a band," Buck said.

"Yeah? What kind of music?"

"All kinds really," Don added, excitedly, "we like classic stuff like the Beatles and the Stones, and . . ."

"Man, that's all you hear on the radio these days," Roosevelt opened a drawer and pulled out a knife.

Buck and Don looked at each other. "We like new stuff, too, like Prince and Bruce Springsteen and . . ."

"Never heard of 'em," said Roosevelt. "But the gospel

community is pretty closed, you know, we kind of get into our own thing and stay there, and if you ask me that's part of the problem." He paused. "Of course, you didn't ask me, but you know Sam Cooke started changing all that and it's an exciting time now, there's all sorts of changes that are gonna come, you bet, not just music, but with everything."

Buck and Don gave no response. They seemed exceptionally pale, Roosevelt thought, even if summer was over. "Hey, you guys haven't told me if you want something to eat. You look like you could use it."

"Uh, sure, maybe, I mean, normally I'm a vegetarian," Buck said, but "since we've been traveling . . ."

"A vege-what?" Roosevelt laughed. "No wonder you look like you're gonna faint, let me fry up this chicken, you'll love some good Southern cooking. I've been to Detroit before, great city, never Chicago though." Roosevelt began placing pieces of chicken in a pan on the stove. "No harm meant, but I could just tell you guys were from out of town." He chuckled again. "Sleeping in a Piggly Wiggly parking lot in the middle of Memphis. In *that* car." He paused, turning serious. "It's okay, though, I don't know how hip I'd be to Chicago ways, first-time through." Then he reached into the refrigerator and pulled out a bottle of Pepsi, 16 ounces, knocking the cap off with a bottle opener, and took a swig. "Don't let all this beer go to waste now."

Don reached in for a couple Dixies and handed one to Buck.

"Now after we're done eatin', I have to get back to the piano, put the finishing touches on a song I'm workin' on, something I'm auditioning down at Stax tomorrow. Have you heard of Stax?"

Don piped up, "Oh, we love, Stax, we do a bunch of Stax songs in our band, stuff like "Can't Turn you Loose" and "I'll Take You There.""

"Really?" Roosevelt asked, surprised. "Never heard of those tunes, but this one I've got going, it can be a contender if I iron it out. There's this up and comer down there, Otis Redding, that needs material, I'm told. Anyways, after we eat, I have to work on it, but y'all can make yourselves at home."

They sat down at a folding table, paper plates on a checkered tablecloth. Buck ate his potato salad, but picked at the chicken without eating much, moving it around his plate. Don dug in and polished off a wing and a drumstick. Roosevelt, a decidedly stockier man, outpaced them both.

The metal fan's steady hum filled the room, but after what seemed like a long time, Buck broke the silence.

"Uh, I hate to ask this, but is it safe to go outside?"

"What, you going for an evening stroll?" Roosevelt chuckled. "It depends on which way you turn. It's a colored neighborhood, mostly, but . . ." he paused, turning serious, "I guess you don't know, it is different up north. See, if we were down at the Peabody or somethin', they wouldn't allow us to be seen together. But, like I said, change is coming; you can feel it, that's one of the good things about places like Stax, shows blacks and whites can work together." He paused again. "But, I'm sorry, I'm getting all preachy now, like I'm in church and that ain't 'til Sunday."

With that, Roosevelt wiped his hands on a napkin and excused himself to the piano, voicing those chords again, and picking up where he'd left off the previous evening.

Buck motioned to Don to follow him into the bedroom and they stole away while Roosevelt hummed and plunked, lost in his song. They flipped on the light and closed the door.

"Is this guy crazy or what? What did you get us into coming here?" Buck exclaimed, in the loudest whisper he could muster.

"He was probably right; it probably wasn't safe in that parking lot." Don answered. "Are you okay? You're sweating like a pig, Buck."

Buck continued. "He keeps talking about our strange car and how blacks and whites need to live together and he says he's going to Stax for an audition, but it's been closed for ten years! Remember earlier tonight, when we pulled into town and went down to McLemore? It was an abandoned building and an empty lot!"

"Yeah, well . . ."

"And look at this place, everything is vintage! Vintage shirt, vintage hat, vintage coffee table, vintage table lamp. Look here," Buck pointed to the nightstand in the bedroom. "He's even got a vintage *Life* magazine on the bed stand. It's weird."

Don had one ear cocked to the side. "Hey listen to what he's playing. Isn't that one of ours?" He was referring to the covers their band played.

I'll be the moon when the sun goes down,
just to let you know that I'm still around.

The plaintive melody trickled through the door. "He's got a good voice," Don observed, calmly. "He should be a performer, not just a writer."

It was all Buck could do to keep from shouting. He picked up a piece of white cloth from the end of the bed and mopped the sweat from his face. "But, he thinks *it's a new song*. And, he'd never even heard of those other Stax hits. Otis is an up and comer? Otis Redding has been dead how long now? This guy is living in his own world. I don't know how I'm going to get to sleep tonight. I'm going to be worried about getting axed or something."

"Hey, man, you just wiped your face with a diaper," Don said, pointing to the stack from which they'd come. "It's okay, they're clean," he added, reading the newfound horror in Buck's face.

Don was still listening to the music coming from the other room. It was some other song now, some spiritual he didn't recognize. "He's got good energy, I can feel it. So what if he's a little wacky, all we got to do is thank him for our hospitality and be on our way in the morning." He shook his head slowly. "Man, he can sing. I wish one of us could sing like that."

This only made Buck more agitated. "Can we sleep in shifts?"

Don shrugged his shoulders. "Sure, if it makes you feel better."

"All I wanted to do was visit Graceland."

"We'll get there tomorrow, Buck, no sweat."

"We better go back to the kitchen before he thinks we're gay or something."

Buck was so nervous and self-conscious, Don sometimes wondered how he ever got into a band in the first place. But, maybe that's why he got into a band in the first place, he mused. And, he was a bass player, which explained a lot in and of itself. As they walked back into the main living area, Don eyed the telecaster propped up against Roosevelt's piano. Now, that was a vintage something he'd love to have.

Roosevelt got up early, around eight a.m. The first noises of the day trickled in through the open window, cars and busses, squeaky brakes and honking horns, bits of Saturday waking up. Autumn was finally on the breeze, and Lord, he was thankful for that. He started to set about quietly making breakfast, getting out a frying pan and opening the refrigerator for some eggs. There were still four Dixies in the refrigerator, and he thought about taking them down to Stax, but then he remembered they didn't drink in the studio either. Over on the couch, one of the boys woke up and lifted his head, and the other soon followed, propping himself up on the floor with his elbows.

"Hey sorry, men," he said, "this is a small joint, hard not to clatter. Want some eggs and coffee?"

"Sure," Don, the long-hair, piped up, energized and ready to go.

"Scrambled is all I do. Hope that's okay." No answer. "What y'all got planned today?" Roosevelt asked. "Going to Overton park? Beale Street tonight?"

"We were thinking of going to Graceland." Curly-headed Buck wiped sleep from his eyes with his palms.

Roosevelt broke an egg on the side of the pan. "Ah, Elvis fans, too. Well, that's cool, we like Elvis down here. But, all you'll be able to do is drive by, they always have someone at the gates."

"We were hoping to take the tour," Buck continued.

"What are you talking about? You personal friends?" Roosevelt chuckled again, a friendly ha-ha-ha they were growing accustomed to, and stirred up the yoke with his spatula. "I was reading where he's out in Hollywood right now anyway, doing another one of those jive movies. Lord, what a waste." He dropped some chopped onions into the pan. Buck shot Don yet another sidelong look while Roosevelt peered into the pan and stirred.

"I *like* onions," Don whispered. Buck's shoulders collapsed, exasperated with his partner's overabundance of cool.

"If you boys don't get in the way, you're welcome to come down to Stax with me."

Don answered yes for the both of them. Buck kneed him surreptiously.

"It's business now." Roosevelt kept stirring the eggs. "But I'll be glad to have some company. They start early down there, so we don't have long."

As it was, the boys barely had time to wolf down their food before leaving the apartment. This bothered Buck immensely; he missed his daily shower and as such felt dingy and scuzzy, his curly black hair matted to his head like a greasy brillo pad. As they pulled out into the street to follow Roosevelt, Buck pulled a little bottle of cheap aftershave from his overnight bag and lifted his shirt and splashed it around his torso to hide what he felt must have been an intense smell. He did this for his own self-image, but in the back of his mind thought, well, there could be girls at the studio. In response, Don, who was driving, raised his right arm and fanned his armpit at Buck, laughing.

Buck held his nose. "Look at his car," he said, as they turned a corner and saw it in all its glory, "that's beyond vintage, that's gotta be from the 50s."

"Galaxy, isn't it?" said Dan. "It doesn't look much older than most of the cars around here."

"It's a poor neighborhood." Buck studied the scenes they were passing. "Some things never change, our man Roosevelt is talking about a change gonna come. Some things change, some things don't, I guess." He looked out the window at some black boys and girls playing over an open fire hydrant. They rode in silence for a moment. "Why did you jump at this chance for us to follow him down, anyway," he asked, "so we could share his embarrassment?"

"I don't know," Don said. "It seemed like an opportunity." Of the two, he was the compulsive one. It always helped in a band to have a songwriting team where one guy was the levelheaded McCartney type, like Buck, and the other was the crazy do anything Lennon man, like Don. "And, we don't know, maybe there's some new Stax around there we didn't see, they're bringing it back somewhere or something, maybe that's what he's talking about."

Buck reached over and hit a button on the radio. A fast-talking dj who sounded something like a Southern Wolfman Jack came on and started rapping about a big sale down at Lansky's on Beale, an upcoming show at the amphitheater, and the latest hit by the Beatles, the fifth number one that year. The familiar opening chord of "A Hard Days Night" rang through the air.

"I have to admit," Don said, a slight quiver in his voice, "this is starting to weird me out a bit. Have you noticed that we haven't seen a single car that looked newer than 1964?"

"Yes, I have, it's like we're down in Cuba or something."

"And this guy on the radio, he's not like an oldies guy; he's talking present tense . . . and all the lettering, . . ." Don's old day gig was as a graphic artist. He pointed to a barber shop sign. ". . . it's all old-time sixties fonts."

Just then, Roosevelt's car slowed down in front of a corner grocery store and the boys looked to their left and saw 926 East McLemore Avenue, reborn from the night before, its movie marquee proudly staking claim to SOULSVILLE USA, in all its glory. Next to it was the shop they'd read so much about in their youth, Satellite Records, with bright hand-pressed posters in the window advertising local shows and racks of LPs and 45s visible inside.

A bus stopped at the other side of the street and three black teenage girls got off, skirts billowing in the wind as they hurried into the record store. A sandy-haired white man with a goatee, tan slacks, and black boots walked into the front entrance of the building. Another black fellow, porkpie hat squashed onto his head, hurried out of the grocery store and across the street to the studio, carrying a thin square box in one hand and a notebook in the other. Like the cars and Roosevelt's apartment, everything was vintage, and the air smelled indefinably different to Don, somehow sweeter, effervescent.

"Everyone dresses like our parents here," Buck said, "only hipper."

It was like being in a black and white movie, except for the color splashed on everything from the posters on the record store window to the different shades of faces entering the studio to the sun already beating down and bouncing off the chrome bumper of Roosevelt's car. The neighborhood was coming to life and Stax was the cup of the coffee easing folks into the day. Don and Buck followed Roosevelt across the street and through the front door. Another black girl with a hoop skirt, heavily processed hair, and big bright eyes passed them and said hello to their friend. It seemed as if she worked there, or at least knew Roosevelt. Buck turned and watched her walk outside the building. He could barely see her calves, but her eyes had impressed.

Once inside, they entered Stax's main studio, a large space with high ceilings and a slanted floor. A drum kit, a couple of Fender amplifiers, a Hammond organ, and a Wurlitzer electric piano were set up around the room. Microphones on heavy stands were scattered everywhere, and large baffles hung from the walls. The guy with the goatee and short cropped hair they'd seen outside sat on a chair at the far or "high" end of the room, aimlessly plunking a bass. Behind him was a glass partition and, on the other side, a recording console and giant wall-sized playback speaker. There was a figure moving beyond the glass, and soon he came around to greet them.

"Hey, Steve." Roosevelt gestured with his hand. "These are two friends of mine who tagged along, they're out-of-towners. You don't mind, do you?"

"No, man, as long as they don't make trouble," he replied, deadpan. He had bright blue eyes, a D.A. haircut, and an affable, eager to please demeanor. "Where you boys from?" he asked. Don answered.

"Chicago, ahh, bluesland," Steve drawled, ever so slightly. "Welcome." He looked around the room. "We're just doing auditions right now, so feel free to sit down," he said, motioning to a row of four metal folding chairs.

They did so, as Roosevelt and Steve headed back behind the glass. "Is that Steve Cropper?" Don whispered.

"Steve Cropper's an old guy with a beard and a ponytail who doesn't do anything anymore but play with the Blues Brothers," Buck said. "That guy is younger than us."

"But, look, he's got an old vintage telecaster, and over there," Don said, excitedly, "that's a B-3. Maybe that's Booker T's."

Soon more people filed into the room and began milling about, chatting in groups of twos or threes. Many of them seemed to know each other, mostly young men, black and white, their "uniforms" being versions of the clothes they'd seen inside and out, turtle necks, striped short-sleeved shirts, tan slacks, black boots.

The cute girl in the hoop skirt and sleeveless blouse came back in, and Buck kept on eyeing her. Don noticed, and thought, man, can't he just exude a little cool, for once? He wanted to let him know he'd read once that people can tell when they're being checked out; it's like a sixth-sense. Sure enough, the girl turned around and looked in their direction and just then another man came in and blocked the view, shouting, "Carla, what are you doing down here on a Saturday?" "Waiting for you, Al," she said with a laugh. "Oh, you're bad." They hugged and then he laid a couple drum sticks on the kit, and left the room again.

There was a feeling of family in the air. Roosevelt returned to the boys.

"Hey, guys, it'll be a few minutes. I've got to wait my turn, and Otis isn't here yet anyway. The whole band will be down in a bit."

"Is that Steve Cropper?" Don asked.

"Sure is, you know him, too?" Roosevelt laughed. "You boys kill me. Listen, I'm going across the street to get a soda, you want anything?" They nodded no. "Okay, behave yourselves."

Don was itching to go over to Steve and ask him if he could play that telecaster. "Did you see that girl," Buck whispered. "She's cute." Buck was suddenly no longer worried that the cars were old and that everyone dressed funny.

A new arrival came into the studio and shouted, "Hey,

whose weird-looking car is that out front? You driving that buggy, Duck?"

"Nope," the bassist replied. Bass players, thought Don, doesn't matter where you are, they're all the same. "It's ours," he volunteered.

This fellow was dressed a little slicker than the rest, with a black sport jacket, dark ray-ban shades, and an Afro that seemed to grow out just a little more than everyone else's. He took off the shades and came over to where they were sitting.

"Wild, man." He extended his hand, and they shook it in turn.

"My name's Booker." He surveyed their t-shirts. "You guys from out of town?"

"We've got a band, up in Chicago, and you know, we're huge fans of yours," Don rushed along. "We have all of the MGs records and we do some of your stuff, like 'Green Onions' and 'Time is Tight' at our sound checks and, well, in our sets, sometimes, too, and . . ."

"Really? I didn't think too many people north of St. Louis heard what we were cutting here . . . but I appreciate that." Booker started walking over to his B-3, muttering, "'Time is Tight,' is that ours? I don't remember that, but . . . good title . . . ," sitting down to trade licks and riffs with the bass player.

Steve came back in the main studio and started getting things going; he was obviously the man in charge of the sessions. Once people started auditioning, it went quickly, but most of it was dull. The singers were good, but the songs were just okay and a lot of them were overwrought, studied, or very simple, as if they were indebted more to the music of the 1950s than the 1960s. There were several 1-3-4 songs, too, without much melodic imagination. Although Don was lost in the magical vibe around him, the material was not what he'd expect from soul music's finest city. Occasionally Booker would play from some sheet music handed to him, while the writer sang his or her song. Sometimes the writer strummed on Cropper's telecaster, making Don green with envy. Roosevelt and the girl in the hoop skirt came back into the room and sat down in the empty chairs to the left of Don.

Buck reached over, and for the first time since they'd entered the studio, spoke to someone new. "My name is Buck, I'm in from Chicago," he said, extending across Don and Roosevelt.

"Carla," was all she said, smiling weakly.

Roosevelt shot a glance to Don as if to say, "Oh Lord." He looked at his watch.

A song or two later, there was a clamor of activity and laughing from the control room. Duck (Dunn, the bassist) and Al (Jackson, the drummer) rose and gave bear hugs to a black man in a cowboy hat and a suede coat. Apparently, he'd just arrived, accompanied by another fellow, white, sporting a Beatles' haircut and horn-rimmed glasses. When they entered the studio, they didn't announce themselves, but nevertheless, all activity ceased.

"Otis!" Steve rushed forward to greet him. "What's up?"

"You tell me," Otis replied with a smile, taking off his hat, "you got me out of my hotel bed early to get me down here to hear somebody's song."

"This man here says he's got your next hit."

"Let's hear it then."

Don felt the whole atmosphere of the studio change the minute Otis walked in the room, it was an energy, a lifting of spirits, an air of possibility. It was the indefinable "it" that many talk about and is, in reality, very rarely seen or experienced. The other man, presumably a business associate or manager, stood in the corner, silent. Otis leaned on Booker's organ, waiting, relaxed and welcoming.

Roosevelt sat down at the Wurlitzer, lifted his hands into the air, set them down on the keys gently and began to play. Don said a prayer to himself, giving thanks for the vivid dream or inexplicable reality he knew he was about to experience. Looking to his side, he saw Buck as distracted and dreamy-eyed, no longer nervous, but with other things obviously on his mind. Bass players, thought Don, that's why they stood in the back.

Roosevelt went out of the verse and into the chorus, and he was working it, hitting that piano harder and pushing his voice to get it over. He had to have balls of iron to play this song cold for Otis Redding, it didn't matter if, at this point in time, Otis wasn't huge yet—it was clear he would be.

> *That's how strong my love is, oh*
> *That's how strong my love is.*
> *That's how strong my love is, baby, baby.*
> *Yeah, mmmm, that's how strong my love is.*

Otis suddenly held up a hand, stopping him. Don feared he might be rejecting the song. But, that would be impossible, wouldn't it? Or, like players in some old science fiction television show, had their appearance here upset the continuity of time and thrown history off its course? "I've heard enough," Otis said, "let's cut this one as soon as we can. You cool with that Phil?" Phil nodded.

Steve smiled and shrugged. "Fine with me. Let me just talk to the rest of the auditions we had scheduled, ask 'em to come back next week." And so he did. And, in no time at all, Don, Buck, Roosevelt, Carla, Phil Walden, Otis' manager, and Jim Stewart, the founder of Stax and producer of the session who had come down to the studio on Steve's call, sat in the tiny control room behind the glass, transfixed as Otis Redding sang his version of "That's How Strong my Love is" all the way through, for the very first time. The MGs—Steve, Al, Booker, and Duck—played impeccably behind him; they were like painters of sound, dynamic and yet tasteful. There was no horn section present, but Steve said something to Jim about adding that later. The depth of emotion in Redding's voice moved Don immensely. When he reached the choruses, the great singer closed his eyes and held the mike as if performing in front of one, or a thousand, wrenching meaning from every syllable of the lyric.

As Otis sang, Don hung on the lyrics and thought about every boyhood crush he'd ever had, all the girlfriends he'd dated, and who his wife of the future might be. Otis rode the peaks and valleys of the tune with his voice and Don remembered the reasons he started playing guitar and writing songs in the first place, and how he'd hope to one day pay a small part of that debt back, the joy and promise music had given him. Then, Dan thought about how in a world so wrought with conflict and sorrow, there could still be so many things of healing and great beauty. And tears began to run from his eyes; he faked a quiet sneeze, wiped them dry, and soon, much too soon, the take came to an end. For some reason unbeknownst to him, Otis suggested they do it again. And, again. And, after that third time, all parties agreed they had a keeper. On each take, however, Don vainly fought away tears.

Everyone was silent during playback. Afterwards, Otis and his manager shook hands all around and left quickly, taking the wind out of the room.

"I think we got a hit," Steve said to Roosevelt.

Don was nearby. "Oh, do you ever. The Stones will have a hit with it, too." He blurted out excitedly.

"The Stones?" Roosevelt laughed. "Whatever you say, man." He continued, "Hey we're all going out for some barbeque, you want to join us?"

Don declined the invite on their behalf and thanked his host for his hospitality. While he was normally game for anything, he felt that in some intuitive fashion, they'd pushed their luck as far as it would take them.

"No sweat, you were my good-luck charms." Roosevelt took out a piece of paper and scribbled. "Here's my number, look me up next time you're in town."

Don took it and told him they would. As they headed out of the dark studio and back into the sun, Buck whispered, "Why are we leaving now?"

"I thought you were freaked out." Don lied just a little. "And I didn't want to overstay our welcome, you know . . ."

Out on the sidewalk, Buck popped his head into the record shop. Carla was there, working the counter. "Bye," he said.

Bass players, thought Don, they never learn.

As they approached their car, Don tossed Buck the keys. "Your turn." He pulled the map out of the glove compartment. "What do you think? Graceland?" Don felt strangely at ease considering the turn of events he'd just experienced. There was something infinitely clear about having reality stripped down to its basics, in this case the simple fact that he was in Memphis with his bandmate at some indefinite moment in time different from the one he was used to. It was a short drive to Elvis' house and the boys were quiet along the way. It didn't take long for them to realize nothing had changed. The street sign read South Bellevue Road, not Elvis Presley Boulevard, as it would later be renamed. And Graceland was where it would always be, but without the gift shops, tour uses, and post-mortem exploitation. It was just a big mansion with a guardhouse and famous double gate at the entrance to the drive, all decked out with musical notes. A few flowers and gifts to the King were laid on the sidewalk. Whether Elvis was at home or in Hollywood, it was clear that he was most definitely alive.

Buck spoke first, "I don't know man, this is still too weird for me. I say we head home. We could take turns driving and get there by early morning."

"You don't want to stay here?" asked Don

"What do you mean?"

Don had been thinking about other things as well. "Well it'd be kind of cool to be stuck here in 1964, you know, we could get our foot in the door at Stax, maybe get some songs cut . . . maybe do some sessions."

"Are you crazy?"

"We could invest in all the right inventions, you know anticipate the stock market and stuff," Don continued. "It seems like a sweet deal to me. And we've already got our in."

"And what about our families, and our friends, and the future of the band?"

"And what about Carla?" Don said, pushing the button.

There was a long pause after this. They were approaching the lights of downtown Memphis. Buck pulled over at the side of the road and put on his hazards. "How about this?" he said, "how about we start driving back to Chicago, if we get there and it's still 1964, we come back here and work our connections. If we get back to 1984, from where we came, then that's how it was meant to be."

Don couldn't argue with the logic, so he agreed to the deal, although secretly, he was banking on a permanent time warp. On the way home, they took turns, one sleeping while the other drove, and then reversing the trend. When Don was behind the wheel, he put in *Otis Redding's Greatest Hits*, played both sides, back and forth and then repeated the song they'd seen cut, at least three times.

I'll be the weeping willow drowning in my tears
You can go swimming when you're here
I'll be the rainbow when the sun is gone
Wrap you in my colors and keep you warm

After awhile, Don put his hand to the window and felt the cold. Winter comes early in Chicago and he pulled off for gas as they reached the outlying suburbs. Gas prices were high. The Tribune had a headline about something President Reagan was doing. He switched on the radio and it was all Prince and Springsteen. They were back.

Don and Buck never told the rest of the band what had really happened in Memphis; they figured they'd never believe it. But the memory stayed with them and sometimes on tours, if the other guys were sleeping, they'd talk about it a little bit, in hushed tones, and in cautious code, like "remember Otis?" They played Memphis several times over the next couple of years, and they'd always take time to go around and sightsee. Elvis's empire grew and shrank and grew, and the Piggly Wiggly disappeared. The Peabody Ducks kept walking through the lobby and the heat beat down on the city streets, as it always does. They'd drive by McLemore

Avenue to pay homage to the great soul music that came from that site. The whole band would get out and stare at that empty lot and say nothing, while Buck and Don's thoughts circled around and around.

The band toured the country quite a bit, made one record and then split up. Buck started a little record shop that sold vinyl and reefer paraphernalia. He'd loosened up enough to recognize where his real profit margins lie. But, he lived in a small conservative town and the cops busted him and he was stubborn about it and even did a little jail time. He got out in a few months and though they'd grown apart, Don would come in from time to time and play backgammon while they listened to Otis records. It was their little way of staying connected, he supposed. But, it wasn't enough, because a few months after Buck got out of jail, he hung himself.

Don kept playing music, though he decided it would be easier to do as a solo artist, either slinging his guitar by himself or hiring musicians to back him as a tour or session would necessitate. And, he kept visiting Memphis, and he kept visiting McLemore. It had special significance for him now, because he was visiting not just for the music, and the memory of Otis, but also the memory of Buck.

Twenty years after the time that they'd gone back in time twenty years, Don showed up at McLemore one day to find that Stax/Volt was back. Someone with vision built a museum and music school on the former site, perfectly recreating the marquee and the old record shop, right down to the lettering on the side of the brick wall facing College Avenue. He pulled up behind the center, parked his car, and bought a ticket to take the tour. As he was doing so, an eager lady behind the counter pointed to a little theater on the left and said "you'll want to see the film, it'll give you all the inside story." Don thought of many things to say, but simply thanked her, entered the theater and sat in the dark by himself, waiting for the film.

It began with a soundtrack of great soul music, interspersed with commentary from all those involved in the label and studio's beginnings—Steve Cropper, David Porter, Booker T—faces etched in Don's memory, from books, and of course, his experience of many years ago. Then there was live footage, the MGs, the Mar-Kays, and Carla Thomas singing "B-AB-Y." Don thought of his old friend Buck. And, finally, there was some grainy black and white footage of the late Otis Redding singing a song in London before a live audience, the same song that Don heard recorded so many years before.

> *I'll be the ocean so deep and wide*
> *I'll get out the tears whenever you cry*
> *I'll be the breeze after the storm is gone*
> *To dry your eyes and love you warm.*
> *That's how strong my love is.*

Don looked around the theater; it was filled with young African-American high school kids, boys and girls on a field trip, eyes riveted to the screen as Otis sang. There was also an older couple holding hands, tourists from Germany, he'd overheard them chatting. Don wanted to stand up and testify and say, that's really how it was, this was an amazing time with amazing people making amazing music. But, he knew that would be foolish, and so, instead, he remained where he sat, in the back row, this time letting his tears fall unhindered. And, as they soaked into the carpet, Don paid silent homage to all the beauty there is in the world and all the good days that can make up a life.

De-tox

LOU—Part One

The phone rang.

"Yeah, as far as I know, the show is still on. I guess Lou took off for the Bahamas and his mom is running the club right now. I heard his dad split, too. Somebody said he's up at Mayo Clinic. I have no idea what for. Peter said the date is good, so I guess that's what we'll have to go by. Yeah, sure, I'll let you know. Bye."

Neil had been getting calls from his fellow band-members all day. They had a very important gig coming up in a week and Neil had guessed they might be cancelled at the last minute. Two days ago he stopped at the club to go over some contracts and Peter dished out the news.

Lou took off for the Bahamas.

Anytime Lou dropped his coke spoon, bands all over the area lost faith in God. The last time he split, a whole month's dates were lost because his dad took over and decided to turn the club into a blues bar. Lou's mom was partial to lounge singers. Lou had a tin ear.

Lou was born in Sicily, but he grew up in Chicago. He ran the place for his parents, and the place featured the latest in rock and roll. It was even called "The Place." Lou wasn't into music, but he had his brother Peter book the acts for him and act as an in-between set d.j. Peter was a closet homosexual and a go-getter in the booking business. It was a smart move. Sometimes Lou would stand within earshot of Peter and cackle, "Hey, I hear the Beatles and the Who had gay managers. They did okay, right? Heh, heh, heh."

Lou loved show business. He didn't know much about

running a club, but he had a latent nag of a mother hanging out and playing video games upstairs at The Place. Occasionally, she wandered into his office to straighten out the books. She looked out for Lou. Or Lou Junior, as he was sometimes called. Peter made a point of referring to him that way.

Neil sat back and remembered the first time he met Lou Junior. It was a cold January night; the parking lot was emptier than Neil's hands. He was carrying a promotional package, a demo tape, and a monthly newsletter, everything but himself. Neil thought he was being businesslike. He asked for Lou, found Lou, and shook Lou's hand. Lou wore mirrored aviator glasses, a ton of jewelry, and a glazed expression that even the glasses could not hide. Neil wound up smelling Lou's aftershave on his hand for days. It soaked right through the promotional package. Anyhow, Neil shook his hand and pitched the band for awhile. Lou listened carefully, nodded his head, and pointed in Peter's direction. Peter took the tape, grinned, primped his hair, and handed Neil a few dozen routine promises. Neil left the club.

As fate would have it, Neil touched base with Peter a few weeks later and the grinner gave the band a break. They drew well and one thing led to another and finally they became a regular act at the Place. Neil thought Peter had a thing for their blonde-haired trombone player, which gave him reason to worry, primarily because he knew they'd eventually have to axe the horn section for financial reasons. Despite that move, the band went right on headlining, and Peter turned out to be a pretty fair guy.

Neil put his feet up and remembered the first time Lou went into de-tox. It was about two years before. Neil wasn't sure who pressured him into it, but if he were a betting man, which he wasn't, he'd lay two-to-one on Lou's mom. She probably got tired of wandering into the office.

At any rate, it seemed to have a positive effect on Lou. The glasses and the jewelry disappeared to be replaced by polo shirts, a trimmed mustache, and a fairly pleasant demeanor. Neil didn't know or care what the guy did in his spare time, but it was obvious that he was cleaned up to the point where he could function on a daily basis. Lou must have given all his aftershave to Peter, because after de-tox, Neil was able to smell their contracts right through the filing cabinet.

Lou took off for the Bahamas.

Apparently he left in the middle of the night, not a word to anyone. Neil never really understood blameless men.

Nevertheless, hardly a week went by when he himself didn't feel like abandoning everything he had for something he hadn't even thought about. He guessed some people were born that way. They either succeeded or seceded.

PAIGE—Part Two

The phone rang.

Mary was married now, but she still called from time to time, to chat about this, that, and the other thing. They were old friends, from an old job. Mary asked Neil when the band would be playing next, and when her voice quavered, he knew she wasn't upset over their possible cancellation.

"C'mon, Mary, the gig's not that important. I can tell somethin's buggin' you," he prodded. "You can tell me."

"Well. . . Paige is in de-tox," she began. "Not yet, but she's supposed to go in next week. She told me two days ago and I haven't heard from her since. Can't get a hold of her."

Paige was Mary's sister. Yin and yang, Mary was always trying to help, but Paige wouldn't have it. Help was more than relative.

"This time she didn't have a stroke or anything, but the doctor said her health was getting worse and they had to get her on some kind of program soon." Mary continued. "This is terrible, Neil. She's only twenty-two."

It was terrible. Neil knew Paige from another old job, the one past the one he knew Mary from. Paige had a couple of strokes the year he worked with her. Or a stroke and a heart attack. Something like that. She used to get laid off a lot, disability, and people felt sorry for her. They'd coddle her, which was okay, but Neil used to wish that they knew what kind of heart condition she really had. Paige was a beautiful girl. She grew up in Baton Rouge, as did Mary, and Neil always pictured them as a couple of Southern belles, though he'd never been south of St. Louis. Paige had a soft drawl that used to crawl out of her fragile face. She walked like a memory.

The last time Neil saw Paige was at The Place. He ran into her after work; he was dropping off some pictures and posters. Neil didn't drink much, so he ordered some mineral water in a tall bottle and nursed it, bending her ear and tapping his foot. They danced a bit, but before long she ran under the influence of some old friends and Neil decided to hit the road. Before he left, he told her to steer clear of the evil spirits. She giggled and dove for the obvious pun, peering wildly into the barrel of her beer bottle.

Neil never understood blameless women, either.

JEFFERSON—Part Three

The phone rang. Neil didn't answer.

Instead, he left his apartment and drove down to The Place. He arrived in a matter of minutes, parked his car at an angle, and hurried inside. Peter slid him a grin and a brisk salutation as he walked through the door.

"Hey, Neil, how's it goin'? You might want to know that Lou Junior ran off with one of the waitresses, which figures. That probably means he'll be back real soon. Good news for you guys."

"Was it Paige?"

"Yeah, I think so."

"Well, I suppose that figures, too."

"Yeah, I'd say so, but his mom likes her, which is cool. You know how that goes." Peter paused to take a cover. "Mom thinks Paige is keeping her boy out of trouble, so she's gonna sit tight on the bookings. Figures Lou Junior will be back real soon, clean as a whistle."

"Cool. Thanks Peter."

Did Mary know where Paige really was? Should Neil tell her? He paused for a moment and thought about it. Maybe someone should tell Paige to tell Lou to go home, so Lou's mom could start worrying again. Neil's mom used to tell him that you can't tell anyone anything. Neil thought this was good advice. Neil was going to tell Peter about it when he ran into an old friend from way back, Jefferson Campbell.

Jeff was a songwriting partner from high school. They went through some bands together in college and now he had an act of his own. Tall and lanky, his personality was bigger than his tennis shoes and twice as rubbery. He had a grin that turned on three corners of his mouth. He used medium-light guitar strings and drank his coffee black. Neil had met Jeff's parents twice and a few of his girlfriends once. The two of them hadn't seen each other in a couple of months, but Neil was aware of his upcoming show.

"Hey, Jefferson, I hear you're going to be doing the Summerfest thing in Milwaukee," Neil began, after shaking his friend's hand. "Big gig, eh?"

"Yeah, it's coming up fast," Jeff smiled. "I'll be ready, though."

"What kind of material are you going to do?" Neil asked, hoping to hear a song title or two he recognized.

"Originals. New stuff, mostly. I'm through with covers." Jeff paused for a chuckle. "The heart won't let me throw 'dem bones anymore."

A tall waitress with a short skirt passed by and Neil flagged her down for a couple of club sodas. Jeff had been through de-tox himself and Neil had seen the temptress of the trade work wonders on the strongest of souls.

"Milwaukee's a pretty cool town, really," Jeff continued. "Did I tell you 'bout the thing with Shadow?"

He hadn't, but Neil knew that Shadow was a rapidly growing independent label out of Milwaukee. A good home. Neil would be more than happy with a deal from them.

"I don't want to get big-headed or anything, but they came to a show and liked some things, but . . . I ended up turning them down."

"You turned them down?!?!"

Neil filled the air with exclamation marks, while Jeff poked at his ice cubes with a tattered straw, running it up and down through his spindly fingers. He stared mournfully at the lonely club soda, lifted his head, and grinned right through Neil.

"I don't know," Jeff began. "I guess I just don't want my dreams messed up. You know, since we've started doing this, I've seen a lot of good bands, like yours, with a lot of talent, go nowhere. Other people, they have nothing and they get popular. I don't want my, I . . . I just don't want to go to school with my pajamas on. Not yet, anyway."

Neil managed a smile. They wrote that song together back in high school. Neil had overheard a conversation in study hall, some kids comparing a dream they all had. In this dream, the dreamer went to school with his pajamas on, oblivious to himself or his classmates. Suddenly, someone would point out the pajamas, embarrassing the dreamer and ending his dream amongst the taunting of wicked classmates.

Neil was fascinated; the dream was news to him and he thought it would make a great song. Together, they left school, heading for Jeff's house and an afternoon of heavy writing. The session went late into the evening, but the song was never finished. Neil eventually became exhausted and crashed on the couch, leaving the tune in his friend's capable hands.

That night Neil had a strange dream of his own. He dreamt that he was sleeping in a big king-size bed, with all his clothes on. He remembered being surrounded by large purple pillows. In his dream, dozens of classmates stood around the bed, in their pajamas, pointing at him and laughing. But he wasn't embarrassed. In his dream, Neil went on sleeping. One by one, the classmates left, and when they were gone, Neil awoke from his dream. He didn't rub his eyes. He felt completely at ease, perfectly oriented.

Blameless men and women aside, Neil understood detox from the day he had that dream.

Falstaff

"I knew Rodney when I was nineteen, if you know what I mean."

Shawn raised his eyebrows and smiled, slyly. He stood in front of the couch, swaying slightly, weight shifting, half-empty beer bottle dangling from his hand. Five of his students sat on the floor in front of him in a semi-circle, cross-legged figures scattered around a glass chair and coffee table. Loud music at a soft level droned like static beneath the chatter of conversation. Down the hall, in the distance, from a bedroom, a television set could be heard, white noise filling in spaces. The party, like most parties, drifted back and forth from one room to the other, occasionally veering off into the kitchen. Shawn's girlfriend, Lucy, rose from the couch behind him, long legs straightening through her well-pressed slacks.

"Anyone need anything?" she asked the group. Two girls paused to shake their heads no; other students who had been listening to Shawn had drifted, oblivious to her offer. She leaned over and kissed him on the cheek, sliding an arm behind him in a half hug, before heading off to the kitchen.

Shawn fell into the couch and turned his attention to the student nearest him, a young man named Eddie, at twenty-six the oldest in the group by a few years. "She's the kind of woman I could picture myself having children with, if you know what I mean. I haven't thought that about anyone in a long time."

Eddie nodded his head, not sure of what he meant, but getting a sense of things regardless. They all respected Shawn immensely as a poet, songwriter, and teacher, for just this vague reason. He was often articulate in his instruction, but even when he got hazy and shot over their heads, there was a mood in his enthusiasm that they picked up on another level, like radar of the soul. "You know, Rodney tried to make a play on her," Shawn continued. "I couldn't believe it, we were out eating at that Mexican place, down the street, what's it called?"

"Lindo Mexico?"

"Yeah, that's right, Lindo."

Eddie smiled, happy he had guessed correctly. It was just like class. "It was pathetic, he was all over her," Shawn went on, taking another swig of his beer, smiling at two girls who rose and headed for the other room. Professor Rodney was another instructor at the university, the one responsible for arranging the professorship for Shawn.

"He's just a brother in the struggle," Shawn concluded, the short sentence transformed into verse as the words were caressed and then clipped, a bruthhhhhher in the struggle. He sipped his beer and waited for a response, picking at the label with his thumb. Eddie stared at the bottle, which read Falstaff. There was a heartbeat of silence.

"Right?" Shawn asked. It was just like class again. Eddie cleared his throat, not sure of the answer.

"Who?"

"Rodney!" Shawn shouted, laughing, draining the rest of his beer and bringing the bottle down on the coffee table. "A brother in the struggle." He laughed again, louder this time.

Eddie laughed too, an echo laugh because he was glad to be the bearer of Shawn's confidences. Most of the students, male and female, liked Shawn personally, as well as professionally. He wasn't handsome or dashing in any preconceived fashion, but his personality shone in a style that highlighted his proud individuality and jagged charm.

The fact is, Eddie wouldn't have been at the party had Shawn not been the host. The second week of class, Shawn came up to him after everyone had filtered out and told him "he had the stuff." He added, "I don't know what you'll do with it, but you've got it." Eddie had always enjoyed writing, but that was the first real encouragement he had ever received. The same day, however, he happened to run into Professor Rodney in the hallway, who spoke in concerned tones about Shawn, saying he was worried about him, that the way he was going "he might wind up homeless." That was the puzzle Eddie was trying to figure out. It seemed as if all the writers he admired wound up full of alcohol and infidelity, lost, and ultimately alone, suffering tragic endings, solitary figures leaving behind flawed and ugly lives scattered with perfect and beautiful words.

A female classmate, artificially tanned and naturally beautiful, came and sat down on the couch next to Shawn. Her blonde hair framed the darkness of her face and eyes in a way that was striking and she had made an immediate impression on the first day of class, her peers alternately thinking, "Who's that girl?" and "Who's *that* girl?" depending. She was wearing a short skirt, above the knees, and as she settled into the couch, her leg brushed against Shawn's jeans and rested there, closely pressed. He reached down to rub her ankle and, then, put an arm around her with great familiarity, asking, "Are you having a good time, sugar?" "Of course," she purred, bouncing up again, skirt billowing as she slipped away to the bedroom, where, by that time, all the students were busy talking through an old movie.

Shawn raised his eyebrows as she left. "Hmmm, fine, fine." Eddie nodded his head and took a sip from his beer, the same one he'd been nursing all night. Lucy walked into the room and picked up his empty bottle from the table, replacing it with a full one. It, too, read Falstaff on the label. "Just like a waitress," Shawn said, patting her on the butt as she walked away. "Later," she replied, eyes dancing playfully over her shoulder. She was not conventionally pretty, but Eddie thought her clear brown eyes and the slight turn at the corner of her cheek when she smiled had a way of growing on any man who could see straight.

Shawn popped open the beer and took another long pull, swallowing hard. "That hits the spot. On the spot, my man." Then, he lowered his voice and motioned to Eddie, who tentatively moved closer on the carpet. "Listen, that one who sat down here a minute ago." Eddie nodded, looking up at Shawn. "She works part-time as a stripper, some club down on Halsted. Really. One day she stayed after class for some tutoring and told me all about it." He cackled loudly.

Lucy was off somewhere tending to the other guests, and the rest of the party was going strong down the hallway. Eddie's foot was falling asleep, so he crossed and uncrossed his legs as Shawn provided more details. "Then, she came up to Washblock," he said, "the writer's colony where I've been staying . . . and she showed me." There was a pause for effect. "Gave a dem-on-stray-shun. Hmmm, " he added, lingering on the hmmm, drawing it out, shaping it into syllables and turning the word into a long line of self-contained poetry.

Shawn was good. He read his stuff to class sometimes and even if they didn't understand all of it, they felt it, which was one of his mantras. Technique is fine and dandy, he'd say, but if it don't have that swing, it don't mean a thing. It can touch your heart or your crotch, he'd add, it don't matter, as long as it hits you and makes you see things a bit differently than you did before.

Eddie noticed Shawn studying the room after finishing his latest story, surveying it with a confidence driven by the moment, and he felt a growing sadness, as if the party had somehow extended beyond its natural climax, that they were now entering pages of a story that should have been clipped minutes before. Shawn was from the South and for Eddie and his classmates, that usually gave his words added po-etry, rising from the land of storytellers, myth, legend, and warm eccentricities, to arrive in their frosty northern town. This time, his voice sounded strained to Eddie, as he cleared his throat and began. "Check out this poem she wrote, or at least, what she thinks is a poem." he said, withdrawing a piece of paper folded in fours from his pocket. It came un-done like a flower, revealing soft blue lines that flowed and rolled gracefully across the page.

"My body aches for you, but I'll bear the brunt," Shawn read. "I want you inside of my soft wet . . ."

There was a crash from the kitchen, and Lucy's voice following.

"Oh shit."

Shawn jumped up and stuffed the paper back into his pocket, crumpled, as he hurried to the kitchen. Eddie fol-lowed.

"What happened? Are you okay, babe?"

There was a puddle of beer in the middle of the floor. A six pack of bottles toppled in and out of a collapsed carrying carton; a few were broken, a couple whole. Shawn took a second to survey the site and her sad face before reaching down to grab one of the good ones, twisting off the cap and handing it to her. "Here, this'll make ya feel better," he said.

She rocked on the balls of her feet, gently, holding the bottle in her hand, looking at him with a smile, not on her face, but in her eyes.

"Drink up, my dear."

She took a swig. Shawn made a funny face, jaunty, subdued and apparently calming. "Go sit down, ya hear, Eddie and I will clean up this mess, right Ed?" He turned to Eddie.

"Sure," he answered, taking another step into Shawn's

inner world. "I'll help." His three words sounded flat and one-dimensional in the air compared to Shawn's soft yet dynamic Southern accent, and he felt odd man out among them in the kitchen.

"Now you just tell us where the bucket is, darling, and we'll get right to it."

Lucy smiled. "It's no big deal, I can take care of it," she said, immersed not in his offer but the simple act of chivalry. "You go sit down and I'll be with you in a minute."

"Are you sure?," Shawn asked, nodding his head in sympathy.

"I'm sure."

"Okay, then. In that case, Eddie and I will sit down and continue our rockin'. But before I do . . . "

Shawn reached down and selected the remaining unbroken beer bottle, wiped it clean on his shirt and then set it back down on the floor. He flicked his wrist and set the bottle into motion, and it spun it in a tight circle, rapidly, finally slowing to a halt with its front end pointed not at Lucy, nor the refrigerator, nor Shawn, but just to the left of Shawn, at Eddie. "That don't mean jack," Shawn laughed, as he leaned over to kiss Lucy. Then, he picked up the bottle, opened it, and took another long drink, swallowing hard, letting out a grandiose belch in the wake of his actions. Lucy shook her head as if to say, "I don't know why, but I do." "After you, my friend," he gestured to Eddie, following him back to the living room, where they sunk into the couch again.

Shawn raised his bottle, drinking heartily, before dropping the half-empty down on the table next to the other half-empty he'd been working on before the accident. "Seems we have a problem here, Eddie," he said, pointing to the bottles, mentally figuring which one needed his attention first, a lazy train of thought that was suddenly derailed by his own demanding, rhetorical exclamation. "What is this shit we're listening to?" Two students about to re-enter the room gave a little start and made scarce, heading back down the hallway without attempting to answer. Shawn shot up off the couch and over to the stereo. Loud guitars and drums were rumbling along in a seemingly endless drone, capped off by a whiny youngster singing about life in the suburbs.

"I think it's the Flying Bohemians," Eddie offered. The music stopped abruptly as Shawn hit the button on the CD player and ejected the band. He laid it on the stack of discs next to the player.

"I can't believe Lucy listens to this crap," he muttered.

Eddie was sure that Elizabeth, the voluptuous stripper slash student, had brought it, but said nothing. "Let's see . . . ," Shawn continued, reading the spines of the CDs, "here's one . . . much better." He looked it over and opened the jewel case, taking out the CD, dropping it into the player, and pushing the button. Angular mandolin chords rang out gently, laced with slightly distorted electric guitar lines carrying the melody, while a whiny oldster sang about life in the cities. Shawn raised the volume a notch, turned around, took a step, and stopped . . . cocking his head to one side, he listened and then pivoted back to the stereo where he reached for the dial and gave the levels a second and third boost. Satisfied, he returned, grinning, to the couch where Eddie waited. "Ain't that the truth, Eddie, my boy," he said, gesturing over his shoulder at the stereo. "He had it right, my man."

Shawn and Eddie sat quietly on the couch, listening to the music. Eddie was beginning to relax again, as if a new story had begun and he was more certain of the ending. Artists were different, that's all there was to it, and sometimes being different meant doing things most people wouldn't dare do, he thought. If we don't go there and experience those things and bear witness to them, Eddie thought, who will? But, more than the lifestyle, he loved the writing process; it was a discipline, but the more time he put into it, the more able he was to pull ideas seemingly out of thin air, as if they'd be handed to him through divine inspiration. No matter how he felt while putting it down, the words came out pure and real, more real than life itself. The process was so intense, however, sometimes Eddie found himself pulling back and wondering whether he could ever really let it fly, like Shawn, without damaging himself.

Eddie lingered on that thought and decided what he really needed was another beer, so he got up to get one, when Shawn sat up straight and motioned him closer. Eddie moved a bit closer. Shawn motioned again. Eddie nervously brought himself almost as close to Shawn as Elizabeth had been.

"You know, that's an old trick," he whispered. Eddie said nothing, blank, waiting.

"You don't know what I'm talking about, do you?"

"No," Eddie admitted, sheepish, drawn into confidence and then lost, parallel to failure. He didn't know the answer, there was something between the lines, and once again, it felt much like class.

"There was no way I was going to clean up that mess," Shawn confided. "See, as long as I make the offer, I'm out of the woods." There was a quick pause, for Shawn did all things quickly as well as suddenly. "See? It works every time." He laughed and picked up one of the bottles, holding it loosely in his hand, swinging it like a heavy watch on a long chain. "Between you and me, bud, between you and me." Shawn reached over and raised his bottle at Eddie, a toast to their complicit camaraderie. He emptied its contents, guffawed, and let out another hearty belch.

Eddie's empty sat on the table, untouched, as he looked past Shawn, over his shoulder to the kitchen, where Lucy was on her hands and knees, sweeping the broken glass into a dustpan. She worked quickly, dumping the contents into a paper bag, reaching for a sponge to get the rest of the beer. Shawn may or may not have noticed Eddie's glance. He leaned back, put his feet up on the table and said, "We're all just brothers in the struggle, my friend. Brothers in the struggle."

Negative Space

The painting was jagged yet smooth, dashes and splashes connected in seemingly random patterns, so beautiful and kinetic that it practically flew off the wall. It was a famous work, and though Ryan had seen reproductions in books, prints, and movies, he had never stood inches from the canvas. He was immediately struck by its power, and as he stepped back to take in its entire length, he saw that, to him, the power came from its negative space, the bits of quiet tranquility that lie between the fervor of the paint itself, falling madly from the artist's vision. For that reason, he immediately connected with Pollack's purpose. He had built his own life on quiet, the spaces between conversation, he lived in those places and sometimes those closest to him complained about it. In the past, some had accused him of keeping his space locked tight, in an area sanctioned from light or positivity.

Leaving the room, he walked around the corner to the café where his friend was waiting. They had begun their day at the Tate together, but she was very fast in all things she did, quick in processing information and moving on and as such, always seemed to be one step or room ahead of him. And, so she was waiting with two lattes, a scone to share, and a table next to the window. Rain dotted the glass, and outside, boats lazily moved up and down the Thames, casting gentle waves in the murky steel gray water. The millennium bridge stretched across the river, its twisting tubular pattern a stark modern contrast to the boxed drab office buildings lining the opposite bank.

"Too bad it's raining, eh?" she said, kissing him on the cheek and sliding a hand along his back as he bent over to greet her. "It would've been lovely to take a sunny stroll.

Hope it doesn't keep the punters at home tonight."

Ryan frowned. He had a gig that night in Soho, and her comments rubbed him the wrong way, because frankly, he hated to think those kinds of thoughts, much less express them. You do your best, and then let the fates take care of the rest, and why think differently, what was the point, it would be a good show, case closed. But, it was odd—back in the states, he'd had gigs where the rain kept people away, and gigs when the beautiful weather kept people away, depending on who was casting the excuse—his manager, the club owner, the girl behind the bar. But here in England, how could the rain possibly keep the numbers down when more often than not it was pissing down?

"It shouldn't make a difference," he replied curtly, before shifting gears. "I love this museum, it's such a great space." Ryan leaned forward in his chair. "I know I go on about that every time I come here, not only the works they have, but the way they organize it."

Julia just smiled and sipped. She had pale alabaster skin and medium-length blonde hair that she tucked behind her ears. She was very animated when she talked and a lock of hair kept falling down the left side of her face, covering one eye, after which she'd reposition it just as feverishly. It was a nervous habit he'd grown accustomed to and liked, because the long hair was sexy and the dark eyes partially hidden and revealed were even sexier. Her silver earrings matched the pendant dangling over the collar of her long-sleeved red sweater.

"And," Ryan went on, "today, because of that, you know, I really noticed for instance, because of the way things are arranged, the variety of styles some of these artists, like Matisse and Picasso worked in. You see samples of their work in every gallery, which shows their range. You know, you go into nude-action-body, there's a Matisse, in the history-memory-society area, there's a Matisse." He spoke quickly, as if to process his thoughts to himself. "I knew Picasso did a lot, in terms of variety, but not Matisse. And it was interesting that they put Pollack, that famous Summertime piece, in the section on landscape-matter-environment, which is a cool way to look at it, particularly when you read how that one scientist thinks Pollack anticipated fractals. That's so wild. And, the negative space in that work, it's just . . ."

"Oh, look, Ryan, isn't that a lovely scene," Julia said quietly. She held her coffee with both hands and pointed her eyes in the direction of the river where a group of schoolgirls had lined up to take a photo on the balcony outside the window, the London riverscape in the background. The girls were all decked out in matching uniforms, spotless white shirts, blue woolen skirts and knee-high socks.

"Yeah . . ." he said, thinking it was just a lark, they probably had to come to the museum for school and in another week, they'd forget everything they'd seen. But he chose to keep talking about the paintings he'd absorbed, and mostly, how they related to himself.

"So, yeah, the Pollack piece had all this negative space. And, I started thinking, I mean, you know, not that I'm in his league, artistically or anything, but I just thought, well, that's always something I put in my music, this idea of negative space. It's something I think I've always done that no one talks about, you know, using negative space, which in music would be silence. And, in a way, that's the same thing that . . ."

"You're quite the philosopher today," she said, interrupting him again. "That's all well and good, love, but sometimes, isn't it better to live instead of talk?" Her smile went on like the rain, but her eyes had turned sad, and her movements slowed down, and together, those actions stopped him from feeling angry. But, he couldn't resist getting the last word in.

"That's a philosophy too, isn't it?" He regretted it as soon as he said it. He should have told her that she should know, and say it and mean it in a good, comforting way. And, he wanted to tell her he loved her, but frankly, he wasn't sure. So he shut up and finished his latte.

They rode the escalator back downstairs and walked up the slope of Transom Hall, hand-in-hand, bridging the physical in an attempt to patch up the holes in their conversation. As they walked, they were dwarfed by the large space that rose up above them, and moving outside, they were even smaller in contrast to the open sky. The rain had stopped, and although it was rather mild temperature-wise, it was still cloudy. There was gray in the water, gray in the sky, and it seeped into him in ways his hat and coat could not shield.

"It's only half-one, what should we do now?" Julia asked, seemingly oblivious to the weather and his mood.

"At some point, I'd like to get back to the hotel, change the strings on my guitar, take a shower." He realized he was avoiding the question, but he liked a certain amount of head room to himself before performing and he might as well start trying to set his limits.

"Didn't you already take a shower this morning?" she said, poking gentle fun at him.

"The water pressure is so weak over here, and I'm so filthy," he said, returning the favor, "it takes many showers to get me clean."

"Very funny . . ."

Truthfully, if he'd had his druthers, he'd say his goodbyes, pick up a copy of the *Guardian*, make some tea in his room, and relax and read the paper—by himself. Then, he'd strum his guitar a bit, round up the rest of the band, take a taxi down to Charing Cross, get the sound check over early and have a good bite to eat, maybe something from that fish and chips shop across the street. She could meet him around then, catch the show, and if she wanted to do something afterwards, that was fine, that was okay. But, instead, with a lack of resolve and, consequently, un-resolved plans, he started walking with her towards the millennium bridge to take them back across the Thames and their tube station. She tugged at his arm, pulling him in the other direction. "Let's take a walk along the river. We can pick up the tube at Southwark and maybe then I can go back and help you shower, eh?"

Ryan arched his eyebrows.

"I'm dead serious," Julia pushed herself into him. "What, then," she added, a twinge of exasperation in her voice. "You know I'm not a slag."

Of course she wasn't a slag, he thought, although she'd probably had three or four steady boyfriends since he'd known her. Julia seemed like the type to have difficulty with relationships, though he didn't spend too much time think-ing about it, because he didn't ask, she didn't tell, and their respective apartments were about 5,360 miles away. Ryan liked it that way, he was still a youthful 28, free and single, taking life in small doses, and moving slightly faster than the barges that crawled along the river beside them.

"Take my picture," she blurted out suddenly, stopping him. "Right here, with the river and the bridge and every-thing behind me.'

"But you live here," he said

"So?"

"And you work across the river, in one of those build-ings, don't you?" She was a police sketch artist.

"That's not the point now is it?"

"You don't want the place where you work in the pic-ture, do you?"

She sighed, as he began to rummage through his backpack for the camera. Funny, he hadn't believed it when they first met, but as she liked to say, she was dead serious. And, of course, after that, he hadn't been able to resist coming back with "how did a nice girl like you get to be a police sketch artist?" Things shape your life, she'd explained, and sometimes one event simply leads to another. And so it was with them as well.

"Okay, I've got it." Ryan took the camera out of its case and blew a speck of dust off the lens. She'd never said more than that, but the words always stuck with him. He wasn't sure if she was referring to their meeting or some-thing darker from her past, though time and experience naturally led him to piece a few things together.

Ryan held the camera in front of his face and began to frame the scene. The barge had moved on. She fluffed at her hair with both hands. "Do I look pretty?"

"Beautiful," he said, reflexively. But, he never pried. In general, he liked people, but they often told him more than he cared to know, particularly back in the states where self-confession was a way of life. It was different with her, but still, he didn't want to stare directly into the sun; it might blind him. "Smile, now." As he looked through the lens, he placed her on the left side of the shot, with lots of the dark river and the gray sky in the center, and the white bridge on the right. It was balanced nicely, unusual, and of course, there was lots of negative space. She had her body cocked to the side a little, red sweater on black jeans. As she bent down to pose, he clicked, and a lock of hair fell over her face.

"Oh, damn, let's do another," she said, tucking the hair behind her ear again. "I know I won't like that one." She rolled her sleeves up and back down again and positioned her body exactly the opposite of how she'd posed before. The sun fought to peek through the clouds and so this time he snapped quickly, taking not one, but two more pictures. On the second, she was moving towards him.

Ryan and Julia continued walking along the river, and they passed a woman jogging, a man walking his dog, and two businessmen in trench coats, simultaneously talking on cell-phones, presumably not to each other. They stumbled across a used book sale, rows of soft and hard covers laid out on folding tables. He found an interesting tome on Gandhi living in London, and bought her a gothic mystery she hadn't read. Two for five quid. Then they crossed under Blackfriars Bridge, one of the ancient stone bridges up river from where they'd started, and turned left on a bit of old cobblestone that turned into a proper walk and led them to the entry of the tube station. They had day passes, so they headed straight for the turnstiles, and he bent down to grab the last lonely *London Metro* left in the rack. It was the free commuter paper and he was lucky to get one at this late hour.

"Oh, the *Metro*," Julia said, noticing. "Let's see if you're in it, eh?"

"Should be, that's what they told me."

They followed the signs to the Jubilee Line, and once at the platform, he turned quickly to the back of the paper, where indeed, there was a write-up on that night's gig, in big bold letters under the "Pick of the Night." There was a large photo of him and a write-up, mostly about the new CD he was out plugging. She moved closer and looked over his shoulder as they both scanned the text. The article said the new record was his best yet, "a narrative wonder, the musical equivalent of Bob Dylan carrying Billy the Kid's gun and riding through Oklahoma on a double-decker bus." They urged everyone to come out to that evening's show.

"Brilliant," she exclaimed. "Much better than *Time Again*."

"I guess," he said, thinking. "Although more people probably read *Time Again* than this . . ."

"Oh, I don't know." Their train pulled up and they got on and found two empty seats together. "The bloke in *Time Again* says the same thing every time, that your songs are full of "smoothly intransit wordstyles." She laughed. "It's so silly, what does that mean, anyway? No one I work with would read that and rush out and see you. This one has a nice picture, too." Julia opened up the paper he'd since handed to her. "People like pictures."

"True," he acknowledged. "But, I don't know, this one isn't exactly lucid, either."

"It's still a good review," she said, cheerily. "It will probably bring some new faces to see you. Besides, remember what you told me, Ryan, that you can't give them power, whether they're nice to you or an asshole, it's us who give them their power. Doesn't matter if it's a critic or someone you work with or . . . whatever." Her words trailed off.

"I said that?"

"Yes, you did, and it helped me a lot," she said, gently squeezing his arm. "It was a difficult time for me. Our stop."

He didn't remember it at all.

"Mind the gap," the automated voice rang out as they stepped off the train.

In the hotel, there was darkness, and quiet. Ryan had made sure the shades were drawn tight and the lights were off. He could see the shape of Julia's chest moving in and out, her breath lightly hitting him as his hands gingerly moved across her skin, the small of her back, the curve of her side and flat of her belly. He traced the negative space, the patterns he knew so well, careful to flow between the ridges, the remnants of wounds that never seemed to heal completely. Several were small fine white lines that would eventually fade into time. Another was raised, piercing and red, and oddly, still one more was a small Z. He moved slowly, but at one point, she turned unexpectedly and his hand slipped. "Oh", she said, as her side arched inward. He pulled his hand back. "No, no, it's okay," she said. "It's okay." And, so, he continued, thinking of nothing but her safety and comfort in his arms, a feeling of selflessness he rarely had, and he realized that was one of the things that kept drawing him to her. "It's okay," she said, one more time.

There were half a dozen scars in all, he'd counted them, many times before, on dusky afternoons and pitch-black nights. He figured he probably knew those scars and the skin around them as well as anyone. Soon he left the negative space and moved towards her calves and thighs. She was breathing more heavily, and he felt her tremble silently. All the while, they said nothing, and this too was a relief, he was glad to be removed from the land of words and immersed in a place where language was something beyond their grasp. And so he forgot about his past, and their future, how they'd met and where they were going, and all the little exchanges of the day. She met his kisses, and his body warmed and they connected and reconnected and after they left those spaces, they fell into sleep. Suddenly, the alarm rang.

"Shit, is it morning?" Ryan jumped up and looked at the clock, which read 5:30. He'd even forgotten he set it; he was disoriented, and, apparently, still a bit jet-lagged.

Julia slipped out of bed, and he watched her thin body move through the dark. "It's evening, luv, time to get ready. I'm going to shower, if you care to join me," she whispered, standing in front of him, lingering for just a moment. And so he looked into the shadows for another foggy glimpse of her beauty. He didn't turn on the light until he saw the bathroom door close behind her.

Old Vienna

My refrigerator at home is covered with postcards, and to tell you the truth, most of them I sent to myself. It may sound strange, but every time I take off on the road, I like to send postcards from the various spots around the country I'd never have visited if I weren't a traveling musician. I used to send postcards to friends and family, but that got to be too time consuming, so I opted for sending postcards only to myself. I've built up quite a collection.

Midway through the last tour, I was in Worcester Mass, following what had become the routine—getting into town early, immediately checking into the hotel, and while doing so, perusing the postcard display on the counter. I bought an attractive postcard of New England in fall from the desk clerk, a Robert Frost poem personified, resplendent with its flowing stream, leafy trees, and bright colors. I didn't want to address it in front of her, so I stuffed the card into my jacket pocket as I left the lobby and headed to the parking lot. After a quick shower and shave, I found myself driving through a countryside that bore an uncanny resemblance to my postcard, searching for what I imagined to be a rustic little folk club with a talking field mouse straight out of an E.B. White story acting as doorman. I never imagined how wrong I could be.

The "Old Vienna," as it was called, was located at the heart of a small commercial district, on one of those town squares that aren't really square at all, the kind that circle like a snake and if you're not careful, spin you around like a top, sending you back the same direction from whence you came. Kind of like my postcards, I suppose. I parked across the street and hurried across the walk, entering a vestibule to the left of the main entrance. A bitter wind chased me into shelter as I climbed the stairs in front of me, guitar in hand.

Upstairs, the club opened into a rectangle with a small stage flush against one wall, about six inches off the ground. Tables were scattered around the room in the vague imitation of a horseshoe and plain wooden chairs were overturned on all the tables, legs pointing straight into the air. The soundboard was crammed into an alcove opposite the stage area, and the wall was dotted with posters advertising upcoming shows and new CD releases. I pulled a chair off a nearby table and placed it on the stage, where I sat down and imagined some of the faces I might encounter that evening. I saw faces from the past and faces from the future all rolled into one, a composite face sporting a large mustache and smiling eyes, with a low hoarse voice and a whisper to his wife that told me that for some reason, I should expect an older crowd that night. Maybe it was the man I was opening for and his traditional folk leanings. The owner had assured me the billing was a good match, but my instincts began to doubt it. Nothing to base it on, really; it was simply intuition, like a trick leg that acts up in stormy weather.

A cold breeze blew in from the open window, stage left, and a dusting of snow fell off the sill. I got up and walked over to close it, slamming the window shut, and in the aftermath, heard footsteps growing louder, approaching, echoing softly through the otherwise silent room. When I turned around, a handshake and an introduction greeted me.

"Hello. I'm John," he said, "Jonathan Large."

He didn't look to be oversized in any way, shape or form, but as I began to introduce myself in turn, he interrupted me by telling me he knew who I was. Apparently, a friend of his had seen an article in the weekend section of the local paper, plugging our show, only it was a full-page piece that focused entirely on me, the opening act, and made scarce mention of John, the headliner. He didn't seem bothered, however, and instead appeared genuinely happy for me, as he smiled and rolled up the sleeves of his red flannel shirt.

"I guess I'll just add you to the list of people who opened for me and went on to bigger and better things," he said with a laugh.

It was odd . . . headliners usually offer little quarter, unless they hang around to see you play (which isn't often) and wind up particularly impressed (which happens even less).

It was unusual for him to even be there at this early hour. There was sadness in his voice, however, despite his good-natured manner, and he was reflecting on his state of affairs as much as mine. I mean, after all, a good piece of press is nice, but it doesn't mean you're pounding the doors down to Carnegie Hall or anything. I longed for a day when I'd be in the position to wish people weren't writing about me. John continued, rattling off the names of some famous folks who'd opened for him, and then surpassed him with their celebrity.

"I'm not complaining," he was quick to add. "I realize my popularity has peaked. The kind of folk music I play is very topical, the sort of thing Phil Ochs or Tom Paxton were known for. It's passe these days." He paused, as if to ponder all the musical changes he'd encountered in his lifetime. "My audience is limited. Small, but loyal."

His honesty was so brutal, it made me uncomfortable, and since we were still standing on stage, I thought I'd change the subject by asking where the dressing room was. He pointed and I followed as he headed back in the same direction from which he came, sending us both down a long narrow hallway, up a short flight of stairs, and into a cluttered junk room that doubled as "the green room." I sat down at an old battered wooden desk, next to where John had laid his guitar, a shirt, a backpack, and a pair of shoes. Graffiti on the wall in front of me carried messages from one wandering minstrel to another, scrawled in tiny spaces like notes stuffed into a bottle. "Greg, I loved your last record. See you in Michigan." Some folks simply signed their names and scribbled a date, marking their territory, their passing. Some of the dates went back six or seven years, and some of the names I remembered from childhood.

John sat down in the chair next to me and opened his guitar case, taking out a rag and a small can of shoe polish. He twisted the can open in one motion and daubed his rag in the polish. Then, he slid his left hand into the left shoe, picked it up, and began buffing.

"I hate going on without shining my shoes," he explained, working his cloth into the leather. I nodded and watched, in the vast wasteland between boredom and fascination. Finally, I asked if he knew when sound check was.

"Oh, probably in about an hour," he guessed.

"When did you get here?"

"Oh, about 5. I took the bus in from Boston." He stopped buffing and looked to the ceiling, calculating in his mind, I assumed. "I left my house around 1, so by the time . . . I think it got in around 4:30."

I had never encountered a musician who traveled from gig to gig on the Big Dog. Some had their own bus, but the Big Dog was another story. It struck a romantic chord with me, as I imagined our forbearers, pioneering figures like Blind Willie McTell and Reverend Gary Davis, riding the buses and trains from show to show in the thirties and forties or before, criss-crossing the country carrying only their guitar, a battered suitcase tied together with twine, and a headful of music. It probably happened that way, in those days, and it was nice to know someone was still doing it, even if it wasn't quite the same.

John turned his shoe over in the dim dressing room light and studied it for a moment. He found a spot he missed and began buffing again, pouring on the elbow grease until I thought he might wear a hole in that shoe. Faster and faster he buffed, as he confessed that he felt he'd been lucky to be able to make a living making music, something many dream of but never achieve, although he was aching to get off the road, it'd been fifteen years now, and while he only played about 70 dates a year, he'd like to do some other things with his life, getting married and having kids being first on the list. When he was done buffing, he stopped talking and picked up the other shoe, repeating the process. Finally, he lined up both shoes on the floor in front of him and pulled a blue flannel shirt and portable iron from his backpack. He cleared a spot on the desk where I was sitting and laid out the shirt, ironing back and forth, one sleeve and then the other, flipping the shirt periodically. Faster and faster he ironed, telling me more than I ever cared to know about the life and times of Jonathan Large. "I hate going on wearing wrinkled shirts," he explained.

My set went fairly well, considering the calls and reservations indicated most of the people in the club had come to see Jonathan. There's the power of the press for you. Anyway, the audience was attentive, they listened to what I was doing, and the songs that usually go over best went over best, and the ones that go over okay, went over okay. When I was done, I headed back to the dressing room, and on the way, I heard one of the waitresses say "nice set." I was putting my guitar back in its case when Jonathan walked in and said "nice work," so between both reviews, I felt pretty good about it all. He towered over me as I bent over my case, and his shoes sparkled in my face, blinding me with their shine. By this time, I was curious as to what his show was all about, so I decided to stay for awhile. I headed back to the bar, looking for something to drink and a place to sit. Coffee was free and it'd been a long week of shows, so I opted to caffeinate properly. After pouring, I ambled over to a space against the back wall, close to where the door girl was sitting on a stool. The room was full, and as I expected, it was an older crowd.

"I liked your set," I heard someone say.

I looked over and saw the door-girl lifting herself off her stool as she spoke. I thanked her and she moved one step closer. She had olive-colored skin and an exotic pear-shaped face that reminded me of a giant tear waiting to fall. I had the sense that she was not a New England native, and my intuition proved correct when we began talking more and her voice rolled along in soft and smooth tones. She wore a white T-shirt with the words "Old Vienna" stretched across her breasts.

"I liked it," she continued, referring to my set. "It was kind of dark . . . reminded me of that guy . . ."

She furrowed her brow, as she struggled to remember the guy's name, the one I sounded like. So many names in the world, designed to strengthen, validate, and somehow differentiate our very individual souls. Out on the road, I tend to forget them all—faces never, but names always. I feel bad about it, but the truth is, most folks have parents with no imagination, and they wind up with names like Bob or Mary. I can remember names like Sebastian and Creshanna. Her name was Anastasia. In any event, I took a stab at where she was headed.

"Lou Reed?" I guessed.

"No, no, it's not Lou Reed, it's someone else. I have a couple of his albums, oh, what's his name?" Anastasia studied me, searching for his name written somewhere on my forehead. "You know, 'Bird on the Wire' . . ."

"Leonard Cohen," I said.

"Yeah, that's it, your stuff reminds me of Leonard Cohen."

I had been compared to Leonard a lot of late and I considered it quite a compliment, although not quite accurate.

"I get that a lot," I told her.

She nodded. "You've got that dark thing going, with the voice and the lyrics and all." She glanced over at the stage, where a waitress was setting a pitcher of water on a crate next to the stool where John would sit. "I used to have all of his albums, but I lent a couple out to an old boyfriend and he never gave them back. The early ones, too."

I knew those albums and liked them, but couldn't resist putting in my two cents, since after all, if the world is a stage, the endless parade of critics must lead somewhere. "I love *The Future*," I offered. "I mean, his early stuff is cool, but that album is tremendous. It says it all."

"Give me crack and anal sex?" she laughed, quoting a line from the title track. It was Leonard's apocalyptic vision, not mine, and under the shadows and soft lights of the club, it was hard to say exactly where she was going with it. She noticed a couple at the door, standing still, looking lost, so she went over to get their cover charge. "Seven bucks," I heard her say. The man sent eye signals to his date, who sent them back, after which he dug into his pants for his wallet, opened it and sheafed through the bills. Anastasia inked her rubber stamp and stamped the back of their hands. John was walking onstage when she returned.

"He looks so neat," she whispered, "like he just ironed his shirt or something."

I didn't have the heart to tell her. He really seemed like a nice guy, and because of that, I sat through his entire set, drinking cup after cup of black coffee, as he led the audience through protest songs and sing-alongs.

Anastasia kept rolling her eyes and telling me how she really got sick of all the 'folk nazis' she was subjected to night after night. She was glad to be getting out of there, and of course, I asked her where she was going, and she told me she was moving to California, to get into comedy. She played a bit of guitar, and to her knowledge, there were no women comedians who used guitars in their act, and she wrote screenplays, too, so she could pitch those while she was working on the live show. Jonathan was playing a song about nuclear waste, and he was getting the audience to sing along with the chorus, which went something like "This ain't Chernobyl or Three Mile Is-land, this is America, this is your land and my-land."

At this point, Anastasia gestured by putting a mock finger down her throat and I had to admit, his agenda was starting to get to me. I wanted to leave, but Anastasia was interesting enough and I figured if she kept on talking, I'd get enough material for at least one song, if not two. She continued and told me she was leaving tomorrow, that this was her last night at the club, that her mother hadn't wanted her to move at all, but when Anastasia said she was going to take "The Green Turtle" out west, mom freaked out and bought her a plane ticket. I didn't know anything about "The Green Turtle," but I soon found out it was a big green

bus that takes people on cross-country trips, where everyone camps out, sleeps on the bus, parties, and just has fun
hanging out together on their way to the coast. It sounded
awful. I looked at Jonathan flailing away and wondered if
he'd ever turtled from show to show.

It seemed a likely thing, for as Anastasia spoke of
turtles, Jonathan was singing a jolly song about irradiated frogs. I told myself that if I hung in there long enough,
eventually, time would pass, and his show, like all things,
would come to an end. My prayers were answered quickly,
as he strummed his final chord of the frog song with great
drama and shouted his thanks to the audience. He headed
for the dressing room, guitar in hand, when to my de-
spair, the crowd began stamping their feet for an encore,
lighting matches and crying "whooo" and "more." Like the
irradiated frogs, they were glowing with new life, creat-
ing a commotion unheard at any point that evening.
Jonathan came back for his encore, and as if reading my
thoughts, sang a stirring version of "We Shall Overcome."
When he was finished, he smiled and waved to the crowd,
shoes still shining brightly in the glare of the stage lights.

Seconds later, I scurried around doing my business,
getting paid, and saying goodbyes to all the wonderful
folks I'd met at Old Vienna that night. I went to the dressing room for my guitar and jacket and shook Jonathan's
hand, with a hearty "nice set," even though I hated it. I
took one last look around the club, surveying, wondering
if I'd forgotten anything, when I saw Anastasia standing
by the door, exactly where I'd left her, waiting for something. It couldn't be me, but whatever it was, I hoped it
would arrive soon. She was better than most, far as I
could tell from her soft words and easy manner and even,
her gentle sarcasm. Sharing some conversation had made
the evening different and more bearable for the both of
us. I headed over to wish her luck and started a "well, it's
been nice" spiel, when she interrupted and asked me if
I'd be in town another day. "No," I said, "I'm off to Phila-
delphia."

I thought about adding a further explanation, but there
was none needed, only the silence of the moment. She smiled
and said she'd like to hang out some more, but she had a
dental appointment early in the morning and a flight to California later in the day. I wished her luck and then handed
her one of my CDs and told her to send me a postcard from
California—the address was on the disc. She thanked me
and said she would. We shook hands. I played in Philadel-

phia the next night—Jonathan was in Worcester and Anastasia was headed to California.

When I got home a week later, I checked the post office box and found it stuffed with postcards. They were all from me.

Another Successful Breakfast

When Sean was young, breakfast was a serving of pale yellow scrambled eggs, lying in a lukewarm heap next to a heavily buttered piece of toast and two strips of crisp brown bacon. On weekends, his mother made pancakes, but every morning during his high school years, this was the breakfast he faced. He'd stare and daydream and poke at the eggs with his fork, doing the math—ten strips of bacon a week, fifty-two weeks a year, times four years of high school totaled 2080 strips of bacon. And, every morning, he would wash his food down with a large glass of milk and a smaller glass of orange juice, taking in the matching design of the glasses, their streaky concave surfaces, subtle and smoky. They left perfect round rings soaked into the napkin that protected the placemat that protected the tablecloth that protected the only kitchen table his childhood ever knew.

Sean hadn't begun drinking coffee yet, though the caffeine buzz might have made for a more successful breakfast. It was dark every day when he was wakened to the sound of Wally Phillips handing out sage advice to frazzled housewives throughout the Chicagoland area, the WGN broadcast peppered with frequent traffic reports and occasional breaking news. Wally's voice cut through the stillness of the house like a jackhammer and traveled down the hallway into Sean's room unhindered. By the time Sean managed to rouse himself, brush his teeth, and stumble down the hall to breakfast, his father was already heading out the door to catch a bus to the train to ride into the city and begin his workday. It was like boot camp, for everyone—dad working to bring home the bacon, mom working to fry it up, and Sean working to try and stuff it down his throat. But, nobody complained.

Eventually, Sean managed to eat enough bacon to get his diploma. Afterwards, he went off to college, marking the beginning of his rebellious period, ignited because Sean had come up with the hair-brained notion that attending a large state school located in the middle of the cold, windy, and gray Illinois prairie was a good idea and that living in a room the size of a jail cell with a total stranger, among hundreds of other total strangers, was also a good idea.

This small town that Sean picked for university was most famous for its corn production, Corn Days Festival, and historical legacy of all things corn. One left the expressway and entered town on a road named after the daughter of a famous corn magnate. The high school mascot was a giant husk, complete with a hairy head that would've gotten stuck in your teeth if it had been skewered for consumption. The community fostered an image of all corn all the time, downplaying the annual autumn influx of lost souls in search of higher education. Sean lived on the eighth floor of one of eight large dormitory towers that rose from the barren flat landscape and reached to the sky like futuristic penitentiaries. They were built out of stone and metal, with a cluster of tiny rooms on each floor, each tower housing 400 students in all.

Sean grew to realize the decision to enroll was a halfhearted attempt to please his parents and give this traditional approach a "college" try. Although Sean had spent his life to that point soaking up burning interests in art, music, and literature, his parents weren't very supportive of those passions. Unsure of how to break free, he wound up in the middle of a cornfield majoring in business, skipping breakfast, running late to class, and sleeping through courses like macroeconomics and geology. Breakfast aside, it was a missing year, ruined by boredom, sadness, and a complete lack of confidence. For Sean, the only redeeming event was when the Boomtown Rats played Cornfest. After the second semester ended, he moved out of the dorms and his parents' house, got a two bedroom apartment with a friend on the north side of Chicago, and in a twist of cruel irony, began eating nothing but Cornflakes with a little sugar on top for breakfast.

Exhilarated by his newfound independence, Sean took the next, essential step and set out to further define himself on his own terms and do what he really wanted to do—become a musician. Sean had played guitar and written his own songs since that fated childhood day when he'd heard Smokey Robinson singing "Tears of a Clown" on the WCFL

Top 40 radio countdown. But he needed the comfort of a band setting to build his confidence, and to play blue-eyed soul with any semblance of authority, he felt he had to find a rock solid rhythm section and a groovy singer with indefinable style. Like so many before him, he put an ad in the local music rag, and the next thing he knew, his band years had begun.

Sean rapidly discovered, as anyone who's ever played music for a living knows, that musicians usually spend more time getting to the gig than actually being on stage. They spend loads of time behind the wheel, or sleeping in the back of the van, filling up at gas stations, and loading equipment in and out of places. They spend loads of time hanging around hotels and clubs, waiting for the rest of the band to get it together, or waiting for the sound man to arrive, and then waiting for the show to begin. They spend loads of times at bars and coffee shops, making drinks last forever by taking the smallest of sips, watching all the people come in and out and wondering how those people have all that time to kill, when, if one weren't on the road, one would be anywhere but in that particular bar or coffeehouse. Some musicians also spend loads of time not being able to nurse that beer, losing control or reliving boredom by design or accident, getting drunk, getting high, or getting laid. This cumulative sense of suspension also gives them the perspective of being a traveler who exists day to day in a world outside of time or the constraints of society.

Sean was a skinny, diamond-studded, double-pierced, tattooed, long-haired nut case compared to the friends he'd gone to high school with, most of whom had finished college and were already wearing suits and ties, heading off to their straight jobs with coffee and briefcase in hand. But, compared to his band mates, Sean was fairly grounded and somewhat conservative when it came to pushing limits, except, of course, when it came to breakfast, a ritual he'd always previously associated with those humdrum high school mornings, a ritual that he needed to recast in his daily quest for confidence.

The first round of breakfasts in Sean's odyssey happened on the east coast when he became hooked on the Great American Greasy Spoon and that most gaudy of late-morning meals, the Hobo Banquet. Sean had romantic notions of the free spirits of yesterday riding the rails with only their destination in hand, and so he appropriately stuffed himself on their namesake, a skillet full of onions, potatoes, and tomatoes, covered with eggs and drowned in hot sauce or ketchup. As for the greasy spoons, they are found across America, but in greater concentration in New Jersey and New York, where the band toured frequently, stopping in at these brightly lit diners late at night or early in the morning. To Sean, they were foggy throwbacks to another time as well as familiar testaments to the present day, and the mere act of walking through the double glass doors past naugahyde waiting couches to a little podium where a hostess swept by with menus in hand and whisked the band to booth or table, amidst the noisy clatter of plates and silverware and streams of conversation, as waitresses crisscrossed the room like acrobats, carrying two or even three plates full of food on their arms, always comforted him.

People arrive in twos and threes at the Great American Greasy Spoon, carrying the newspaper and chattering with each other about some event from the night before. Elderly couples walk slowly and determinedly to their seats, sometimes using canes or each other to support themselves, while toddlers reach for the crayons at the front counter, eager to draw on their placemats. On weekends, in college towns, there are lots of young girls in sweat suits, hair tied into ponytails woven through that little space in the back of the baseball cap, dancing lightly on their necks. Their skin is perfect, smooth as glass, without a trace of make-up. Their boyfriends, if they have 'em, carry stubble and swagger, trying just a little too hard to live up to the scepter of what they've just been through the night before, with that beautiful girl who hugs their arm and sneaks a kiss. And, through it all, the waitresses keep moving, coming over to Sean's table with their brown utilitarian, seemingly indestructible plastic coffee pots in hand, filling his cup to the brim, the minute the level drops down half an inch. Waitresses and their coffee; late in morning, or late at night, angels bringing comfort to what can be a sleepy and disoriented world.

And Sean's band days were like that coffee cup, constantly being refilled with new experiences the minute he drank a little in. The greasy spoons stuck with him for awhile, but then, up north in Minneapolis, he modified his idea of a successful breakfast. The band was doing a show in Uptown, "where you wanna be" as Prince once sang, jokingly pretending they were one of the bands vying for attention in the most wonderful B-movie of them all, *Purple Rain*. "Kid, don't take your personal shit on stage," their drummer kept shouting, over and over and over again at sound check. Luckily, the engineer behind the board got a laugh out of that and when they were finished, they asked her where they could get a good vegetarian dinner, and she sent them to a place called Veggie Trip.

As the band drove down the wide shady expanse that is Lyndale Avenue, they almost missed the rickety brown structure, its wooden façade set back from the street and hidden by two large oak trees. Inside, the Veggie Trip was funky as well; the whole structure seemed to lean to the left, in a vain effort to escape the tide of nature and the times. It was also unusual in that the restaurant served several kinds of veggie dishes, which was really hard to find in those days. It became a regular spot on their visits, and on one trip Sean and their singer went there for breakfast and he ordered a dish of granola and yogurt. Fresh and clean, simple and unusual, Sean immediately switched out his previous home-made breakfasts for this tasty concoction, experimenting with different flavors of yogurt and brands of granola, in the confines of his small studio apartment. And, whenever one of his "lady friends" as Morris Day or Prince might have called them, stayed over for the night, he would impress her by serving breakfast in bed, this healthy treat served up in a silver bowl on a lap tray, with a single rose and a cup of coffee. It was low investment, high return.

From the east to the north and back down south, it was another successful breakfast for Sean, the first time his band played Austin, Texas, as part of the legendary South by Southwest festival. They blocked out an entire week infiltrating the capital of the hill country in a vain effort to gig, schmooze, and rest. The gig went well enough, but there wasn't anywhere near as much schmoozing as they imagined, and of course, with all the music and parties going on, they got less rest than if they'd been touring. But most importantly, it was the week that Sean discovered the joy of great Mexican breakfasts, beginning with huevos rancheros at Juan of the Century, a little storefront restaurant in east Austin that also sold votive candles and large paper wall calendars. Huevos rancheros is Spanish for "ranch eggs," a spicy concoction of eggs over tortillas, laden with cloves, chili peppers, onions, shredded cheese, and tomatoes. They were very hot, and as Sean washed them down with coffee, his whole forehead became sweaty, expelling the toxins of the night before.

Austin was also where Sean discovered migas, at a little joint down the block from the Driskill Hotel. The restaurant was called the Fried Apple and they'd sit outside while they ate, sharing the *Statesman* and watching the armadillo trolleys move up and down Congress Avenue. Sean learned that migas was a tex-mex potpourri of eggs, bits of corn tortilla, black beans, chorizo, cheese, salsa, avocado, and chiles, depending on the cook. Sean asked the waitress for a recipe, to try at home, and the waitress obliged, reminding him that the recipe was flexible because migas is derived from the Spanish word for crumbs.

After South by Southwest, Sean began to attempt huevos and migas at home. His near-north Chicago apartment building housed several Hispanic singles and couples and on one sunny Cinco DeMayo, he invited them all over for breakfast. Some turned up and it turned out to be great fun, Sean anxiously eyeing their faces while they ate, gauging their response and his taste-making authenticity. The responses ranged from "not bad" to "bueno mas, amigo." Sean was so excited, he called his parents to tell them about it, something he'd never done after any of the band's many successful shows. He blabbered on in a string of rushed and excited sentences, explaining the dishes he'd served and the positive response of the diners.

"That's wonderful, son," said his father, who was a little hard of hearing, "they even gave you fees for gas!"

"Migas, dad."

"So, were they all Mexicans?" asked Sean's mother.

He sighed and changed the subject.

Undeterred, Sean's next round of discovery occurred even further east, beyond the diners and across the pond, when the band embarked on their first European tour. It was an exotic world, where they found themselves in pensions instead of hotels, heading to toilets instead of bathrooms, and stopping for petrol instead of gas, at services instead of gas stations. They began in Amsterdam, a city that has an international reputation for debauchery and free thinking. But how does anyone debauch and think freely when all drinking, soft drugs, and prostitution is legal?

In Sean's case, of course, there would always be the matter of breakfast. Sadly, in Amsterdam he found the meal to be, unlike the city itself, rather calm and sedate. The band sat across from each other at little tables in a quiet dining room that occupied the ground floor of the canal house that was their pension. A pot of coffee awaited, and the host or hostess would bring them each a hard-boiled egg in a brass egg holder, a basket of fruit to share, and toast on a plate. They were shown how to prepare the toast, covering it with a strange butter-like spread embedded with chocolate sprinkles. Sean thought the sprinkles might be popular with the ladies, but he never tried this breakfast at home.

The next leg of the tour was in the United Kingdom, and as second cousins to America, breakfast was bound to be a bit more familiar and successful. However, every day Sean was reminded a bit of high school, as the proprietor of their bed and breakfast would serve two eggs sunnyside up, heaping portions of baked beans, sliced tomato, and slabs of unsightly sliced sausage. He didn't want to count those sausages, so he'd wait until the host wasn't looking and wrap the animal part in his napkin, stuff it into his pocket, and throw it into the garbage later. All that was available for coffee was Nescafe instant, and so Sean would drink gallons of it to no effect; it tasted like hot water laced with a melted brown crayon. Finally, he gave in and began ordering English tea, which was much more satisfying and, in a way, set a better tone for the rest of the breakfast. Maybe it was psychological, but he never found a cup of coffee in England as good as what he had in America, yet he never found a good cup of tea in America that matched what was served by his British hosts.

On the way home, Sean stared out the window of his plane as it flew over Greenland, the pilot pointing out the country that no one could see from that height. Sean thought about how he'd felt like that before, pointing out places in his future that he couldn't see. But now they were visible. And the change came because he'd finally had enough time on his own to explore and see outside himself in a way he never had before. Europe had been, if not the final, the most decisive step in shedding the negativity of his childhood and the idea, fostered by loving parents, that one could never be anything different from what had come before, be it in career or cuisine.

To celebrate this coming out of confidence, Sean decided to hold a month of Sunday breakfasts. He'd moved into a loft apartment in the Haymarket area by this time, and if his friends weren't too afraid to venture into his neighborhood, he could accommodate more of them in his spacious digs. Sean began by designing little menus, items to be served, as well as clever clip art graphics, such as eggs, dancing chefs, and beating hearts. Each week was given a title—The Hobo Banquet, The Healthy Beginning, Mex-Tex Jamboree, and Euro Plate. He sent out the menus as invites, well ahead of time, and began selecting thematic CDs from his vast music collection to act as soundtrack for each breakfast.

The month of breakfasts turned out to be a huge success, attended by musician pals, neighborhood acquaintances, a few former lady friends, and breakfast brethren he met through his many trips to neighborhood markets in his search for ingredients. Each week, everyone sat at two long dining tables Sean had rented for the month, clattering knives and forks against their plates, sipping coffee, and chatting excitedly in a wildly eclectic version of, if not the Last Supper, the First, Second, Third, or Fourth Breakfast. Sean received a plethora of compliments for his skills, and more than one guest suggested he start his own breakfast restaurant.

On the second week, one of the clerks from the local market brought a tip jar, to help Sean defray his costs. He was okay with that. Word of mouth even kicked in a little bit, he knew enough about that effect from his life on the stage, and he could tell by the third week that numbers were increasing, as there were returnees and some unfamiliar faces. But, Sean was okay with that—he was as proud of his breakfasts as any song he'd ever written. And, by the fourth week, he was serving a very crowded loft, overfill from the long tables winding up on the couch and chairs in the living room, folks even eating cross-legged on the floor. But, he was okay with that—his dog Marvin scurried around and snapped up any crumbs the minute they fell from the plate.

The fourth week was also attended by his parents. Quite elderly by this time, they slowly moved through the room and sat down at one of the long tables, between a lesbian couple he knew from the neighborhood and a heavily tattooed sound man he knew from the clubs. His mom asked the girls whether they were planning to have children. His dad went back for seconds, while the sound man kept refilling his mother's coffee cup, on her request of course. She was good at getting folks to wait on her, always had been. But Sean was okay with that, too; he was just was glad they'd come to share in the celebration.

After everyone had left, Sean's parents stayed at the loft to drink more coffee and relax on the couch, waiting for Sunday football traffic to die down. They talked about Sean's brother and sister and how things were back in his hometown and what was happening with the yard and the attic and the neighbor who fed the possums and squirrels. Sean could tell they'd had a good time, but they hadn't mentioned either his music or his breakfast, so he wasn't quite sure how the latter had gone down. He was a bit hesitant to ask, fearing a familiar recrimination, or at best, a dark cloud that would taint what had been a wonderful time. But thinking of his newfound self-realization, Sean slid it in anyway, waving his arm at the dishes that lay strewn across the empty table and asking, point blank:

"How did you like the breakfast?"

There was a long pause. His father looked at the floor, while his mother stared at Sean, smiling and saying nothing. Marvin sidled up to her ankle to lick a piece of food off the floor, and she scrunched up her body to avoid contact with the animal. The pause grew longer.

"Well?" Sean continued, pressing.

The old grandfather clock in the corner, inherited from his mother's mother, ticked louder than he'd ever heard it tick before. The elevated train, normally a distant sound from blocks away, roared in his mind as if it was going past the front door. His father got up to go to the bathroom, and Sean kept waiting, knowing no answer was its own answer. His mother was still smiling, weakly.

"My food was cold," she said, finally, "if you want to know the truth." Sean was surprised, not by what she said, but by the fact that her words hadn't hurt him at all, not a whit. He got up to refill his coffee cup, and as he slowly filled it to the brim, he pondered her reply and realized it marked the event for what it was—another successful breakfast.

Caught Between the Snakes and St. Patrick

Send me back home, oh send me back home.
My time is up and there's nowhere to roam.
I been singin' for years and I can't catch a break.
I feel like St. Patrick and I live like the snakes.
I feel like St. Patrick and I live like the snakes.

Slim sang in a nasal twang, to no one in particular, as he waltzed over the river of red carpet rolled out before him. Planes landed and abandoned friends and families, sending them to rented destinations, driving home rented explanations with wild and assorted hand gestures. Slim knew nothing of their dreams; he had some of his own, which at that moment required a dependable van and someone patient enough to help him wade through the necessary paperwork. Twenty-three minutes later, he was ready to roam.

Pernell "Slim" Chance was the unofficial leader of Slim Chance and the Celtic Tarantella, an enigmatic three-piece that had been kicking around the clubs and street corners of Austin for nearly two years. There was a buzz going around on their new CD (*Caught Betwixt the Snakes and St. Patrick*) and as a result, they were invited to a big industry showcase in New York. The time slot and venue were both decent, so Slim figured, what the hell, it was time to walk their talk. Maybe they'd get signed.

Slim was the main songwriter for the band and, consequently, sang lead on most of the tunes. He was tall and skinny and wore the emaciated rock and roll look fairly well. His whole body was a drainpipe, from the long strands of hair on his head, to the pointy AA shoes on his feet. A band of gold shone conspicuously on the ring finger of his left

125

hand; he was the only married person in the band. Slim was a rugged individualist and clung to that marriage in permanent paradox. Maybe it was love. Or maybe it was the years of struggling; broken strings and strung-out romances made for good songs and bad finances. He liked to think he had a toehold on life, being married and all.

Slim's best buddy, Washington Lincoln III, made the big move with him a couple years back, from Albany to Austin. Washington played percussion. Wrapped and delivered in a bongo fury, they called him the Stickmaster Extraordinaire. He wore a soul patch and talked endlessly of Monk and Miles. In reality, he was a short black guy with a closely guarded love for the music of Van Morrison and the poetry of William Yeats. That's where he and Slim held common ground.

Slim met Washington down at the QE2 in Albany. He had been sitting in the back, waiting for Washington's old band to go on, when the power cut and people started freaking. A roomful of cover charges would have disappeared out the door, if Washington hadn't had the presence of mind to grab a flashlight and a set of bongos and take center stage. The crowd fell silent as he proceeded to get gone, banging the shit out of the skins, while "reciting" Yeats' Crazy Jane poems at full volume.

"But love has pitched his mansion in . . ."

Thump. Whack. Bim. Bam.

"The place of excrement . . ."

Pish. Pah. Boom. Boom.

"For nothing can be sole or whole . . ."

Whack. Whack. Bam. Bim.

"That has not been rent."

Bongo roll . . . "ooh, righteous," someone whispered. It was weird as hell and Slim loved it. He wondered how many beatnik chicks Washington had fucked in his lifetime. The power came back after three poems, but for Slim's money, it was the best act he'd seen all year. He introduced himself after the set and a friendship was born, a friendship that would provide the foundation for the Tarantella.

Slim and Washington played as a duo from time to time, but the trio wasn't completed until shortly after their move to Austin. It was a cool spring night, about 90 degrees, and they were busking down on Sixth Street for assorted winos, tourists, fraternity boys, and just plain passerbys. They had just finished playing the Marine Hymn for some soldiers ready to ship out to the Gulf when they spotted a demure ragamuffin girl walking their way. She had a knapsack over her shoulder and a canvas bag that rattled and clanked and buzzed and sang. She started pulling tricks out of the bag, one by one . . . harp, fiddle, mandolin, dulcimer, penny-whistle. You name it, she could play it. She said her name was Jayne Smith, but they didn't believe her. She played some more and they didn't care. Everything she did made sense.

Jayne Smith had literally just fallen off the Amtrak. She was quiet and petite and looked like she might go along with anything to avoid a disagreement. She had a hankering for whiskey, her hair was three shades of red, and whenever she spoke, you could tell she meant what she said. Once upon a time, she had married an investment broker in Seattle, in what was a last-ditch attempt at normalcy. The experiment failed and she soon grew tried of her mundane existence, made more depressing by that city's frequent rainfall. Jayne feared for her sanity and fled for sunnier skies, hoping only that the divorce papers would reach her somehow.

Jayne was the same age as Slim and Washington, late-twenties, but she leaned heavier on the series of couldas and shouldas that littered a reckless past. She vowed Austin would be different and celebrated the change in a song she wrote called "From the Rain to the Riata." The tune, which became one of the Celtic Tarantella's most popular numbers, thoroughly anathematized her ex-husband, former home, and the dark clouds that hung over both. Jayne managed to escape two out of three, but she knew the song could wind up haunting her long after it was written, hanging in her head, holding on tighter than even the most difficult past. Sometimes the rain just kept on pouring.

It poured from the moment the Celtic Tarantella left Austin, as they drove north past WACKO and the Dr. Pepper museum, into the steel and glass jungle of Dallas, a deluge all its own that turned them around and sent them packing, spinning eastward towards Shreveport, showers dousing the flames of the refineries on the outskirts of town, only for a moment, but a moment to savor, especially when driving through Mississippi in the middle of the night, a white guy and a black guy and a white woman between them, WHOA, fried and paranoid from thinking about certain historical events a little too much, until they stop at a MINI-MART for corn nuts, Coke, beer, and two kinds of gas, where the woman behind the counter is friendly and sincere and wishes y'all well, telling everyone to drive safely, but that's impossible, because it's Jayne's turn to drive and she's taking purple hearts with her coffee and Washington can't stop chiding her, calling her "High and Lonesome" and WOULDN'T YOU KNOW IT, it rained all through the night, until they hit Tuscaloosa, where it stopped for five minutes, giving them a window of opportunity that they blew by eating breakfast at a greasy spoon where the cooks used dry-wall tools to fry the eggs and this (or the food) made Jayne too sick to drive, but she did manage to heave on the side of the road, against the beautiful backdrop of the Georgia pines, glistening with MORE RAIN, where Washington got the fine idea he wanted to stop in Richmond to spit on Jefferson Davis's grave, but Slim pointed out he wasn't buried there, so they continued to fight the torrents, floods, and discharge that plagued their humble rental vehicle until it arrived safely in Manhattan, whereby Washington finally proclaimed . . .

"Man, this trip has been wetter than a bunch of 14 year old girls at a Prince concert. Shit."

Washington drummed his fingers on the dash, gauging traffic and working off the rhythms in his head. Slim sat shotgun. He reached for the bag of maps, all arms and legs, as he found New York City, just like he pictured it, and rustled it into shape. Jayne was out cold on the bench in the back. Together, they snaked through the city until they found an unsuspecting parking space for Cal-Van the Tin Can, as their cocoon had been christened somewhere along the road. When they emerged from his guts, like Jonah from the belly of the whale, they were followed by a cloud of stale air, marked and molded by three days of foul body odor. The stench inside that van even made the East Side of Manhattan smell good, which is where they stood, knocking at an unmarked door.

Click, clack, bim, bam. Deadbolts rattled on the other side. The door fell open and they walked through, as sunlight from the street was sucked in behind them like starlight into a black hole.

Beyond the door, black was the operative word, an adjective that could have applied to everything within, everything except the pale brunette with circles under her eyes, stationed near the door. She sat behind an office desk, madly answering a pair of constantly ringing phones. She juggled them as if they were flaming flambeaus and she was standing center stage in a three-ring circus. Slim introduced himself between rings; it was their first meeting, although they had spoken many times over the phone. Her name was Sandy and she was in charge of booking.

Slim sauntered up to the short-sleeved sound man who

didn't give a hang about hiding his track marks and was busy shouting "testing 1, 2, 3" through a P.A. cranked to eleven. Sound check at eight, he advised. It was seventhirty, bar time, the bar clock barely visible as it squeezed itself into one of the tiny spaces poking up between graffiti.

The walls were covered and recovered with miles of graffiti, the trademark leavings of touring rock and roll bands that came and went. They scrawled their monikers on the wall, marking it like so many cats rubbing a stranger's leg. Most of the graffiti was white, in contrast to the aforementioned "everything within." But contrast was not the operative word. Black was . . .

The stage was completely black, complete with black backdrop. The monitors were black, which would match their amps quite nicely. There were two mains hanging from the black ceiling, one on either side of the black stage. They were suspended by black chains, turned to face the empty black room that would eventually be filled with white people, dressed in black. Even the house dog was black, a skinny pup that looked like a Dalmatian with his spots done over, not an unlikely proposition in that neighborhood.

Slim was busy petting the dog and didn't see Sandy put down her phones and stick her head outside the door. She got up and moved toward him and he noticed a look of bored concern on her face. He became worried. Something was up. Something had happened to their van. She said they'd better check it out. They ran into the street.

Broken glass was everywhere; one of the rear windows had been shattered, the door jimmied, and their vehicle emptied. Cal-Van was more or less gutless. Every gig bag, suitcase, guitar, and piece of percussion they owned had been swiped. Only two amps remained. They stood and stared at the wreckage for what seemed like a very long time, until Jayne finally broke the silence.

"I'd be screaming my head off if I wasn't under such heavy sedation."

"This really sucks."

"How are we going to play the gig?"

"We could borrow some equipment from one of the other bands."

"And sound like shit . . . if we even get a sound check."

"It's gonna be tough to get signed if we don't play."

"You wanna play and sound like shit?"

"No."

"We did come all this way."

"So?"

"I don't know . . . what do you think?"

Slim and Jayne continued this discourse for some time, volleying while Washington shook his head and silently scanned the pavement, as if he were examining each and every piece of broken glass.

Suddenly, a homeless man came out of nowhere and started performing a crazed Mayan ritual on the van. He circled it in spurts, all arms and legs, jutting this way and that. He was more angular than a Cubist painting. He shouted out, rapid-fire, words run together like streets on a subway map.

"Shit an' a piss, man. I was sittin' in the alley, takin' a shit AND a piss. Yeah. Couldn't a done a thing, man, jes' takin' a shit an' a piss."

He shook as he spoke, working off the rhythms inside his head. Sweat fell off his peppered brow; his parka was two sizes too big and two seasons too warm for this wet and humid New York City summer night. He inhaled quickly before he resumed, dragging on a big phlegm ball, rolling it around his mouth, and ceremoniously spitting it to the ground. Washington and Slim were in awe.

"I was drinkin' a beer, guys. Jes' drinkin' a beer and smokin' a joint. You know."

The homeless man pulled on his knit cap with both hands, squeezing a well-trimmed afro out of existence. His teeth matched the whites of his eyes and both shone yellow as he pleaded for a better understand.

"Drinkin' a beer, smokin' a j. That's ALL I was doin'. Heh. Heh. Heh. Shitandapiss. SHIT AN' A PISS. They went that way. You know, past the alley, down it, past it, like what did you lose? Maybe I can help you find somethin'. I'll see what I can do. Mannnnn. Shit an' a piss. You know."

They knew he was homeless, because when the van got hit, he let the whole fucking block know that he, in fact, was a homeless man, not a mere thief who hung around the East Village and smashed the windows on rental vans with out-of-state plates.

Jayne snuck back into the club while he was shittin' and pissin', to call the cops, so Slim could file a report for the Budget girl, which might help explain the cardboard window and crushed glass seat covers they would pull up with a week later. The cherry reds came into view about ten minutes after she did so, and shit an' a piss disappeared back into the alley, sneaking off like a mechanical spider on speed.

The cops wasted no time disengaging their clipboards

and writing down a bunch of answers to a bunch of questions. They weren't much interested; to them it was an empty van and another form in triplicate. After they left, Washington remarked that they looked like they would've rather been back at the station, playing cards and telling jokes, eating donuts and . . . takin' a shit an' a piss. Drinkin' a beer. Smokin' a joint. You know. Sounded like a good idea. Washington disappeared back into the black of the club.

Slim stayed outside, parking his ass on the curb in an effort to imitate Rodin's "The Thinker" and figure out what to do about that night's show. He was supposed to be the leader, but he was clueless. All he could do was stare blankly into Cal-Van's silver hubcap (remarkably not stolen), mesmerized by the changing shapes in his own distorted reflection. He felt a hand on his shoulder and jerked back in a start. It was Jayne. She squeezed affectionately and sat down next to him.

"All done?," she asked.

"With what? The gig or the band?" Slim scoffed.

"Neither . . . I meant the cops. Everything set?"

"Yeah, we're covered for the damage. Not the equipment, though."

Jayne knew this already, but her face grew long on Slim's behalf. She frowned and pushed a piece of glass along the pavement with her big toe. Her face was bathed in streetlight and for the first time, he noticed the beauty of her freckles. She turned toward him and let go of a sly grin. Then, she pulled a flask out of her pocket, accompanied by a warm and backhanded compliment.

"It would be an honor to share a drink with the leader of the Celtic Tarantella."

"He's not in the mood."

"It might cheer him up."

"What's in it?"

"Whaddya think?"

"Whiskey."

"Yep."

"Do you carry that thing with you everywhere?"

"Just about."

"You're insane."

"Thank you."

Their banter was quick and playful. Slim had to laugh and she knew it. Whenever he found too much control, she'd lose a little for him. Tighten up . . . limbo down. He grabbed the flask and took a long hard swig. She would've made him take two if he cheated. Rot-gut to him, he swallowed behind watery eyes and a flushed faced. She watched carefully and then matched him second for second. He thought her whole body was going to disappear behind that Cheshire smile. He remembered how much he missed his wife.

Across the street, ballroom dancers in tuxedos and long gowns pirouetted around the floor of a second story loft. A sign advertising the Fred Astaire Dance Studio hung over a row of backlit windows. The sound was muffled but the faces of the dancers were clear and their movements concise, exquisite, a picture of grace. Slim and Jayne watched in quiet fascination, obsessed with the sensual vision above them. Fred and Ginger were very much alive, living in a world untouched by the turmoil below. New York was very far away. A swinging door and Sandy's voice brought them back to the East Village.

"Hey, I just got a call from Sid, y'know, Sid Oberstein over at Polydam. He got a hold of your tape and he's into it. He's coming out tonight."

An urgent message this was, for Sandy was slightly excited, moving into a mode beyond boredom. Sid Oberstein, the world-famous record executive, was a very powerful guy. This could be THE break. The break they'd been waiting for . . . the weight they'd been braking for; it's all the same game, three loner-type kids turning on to something, the whole world breaking wide open and beginning to bloom—spiritually, sexually, intellectually, whatever—pick one or all of the above, or check "other." One moment spills into the other and the next thing you know, there's a whole string of them leading you down a road, starts as two-lane, turns into four, but there's no off-ramp in sight, so you barrel down the highway in a tin can on wheels, carrying lineage traced back to childhood, staying home Saturday night, holed up in the bedroom writing songs or playing guitar or banging on the practice pads, hours on the clock spent listening to, no, studying the 33s and 45s, 78s and beyond, but it's more than coming of age, it's spooky wisdom from the lips of a crusty old blues singer, mysterious sounds billowing across a backwoods porch, out in the swamps somewhere, or in the mountains or the streets of Memphis or San Antonio, far away, in time and space, it starts one place and ends another, could be the sound, could be the smell, or the still air that hangs outside the window and waits, as youth gets sucked up the radiator hose and spit back out, many years later, no, you can't get off the highway, but you never regret it, because even the lows are highs and the whole thing makes for a beautiful ride. The Celtic Tarantella were aware of this, so they cut the bullshit, scrambling and speeding to a decision. They decided to play.

As it turned out, Sid walked in about two "songs" into their set and was amazed by what he saw; a white guy, a black guy, and a white woman in-between, singing their parts accapella while pounding out counter rhythms on sticks and stones. The black guy sounded like he was quoting Yeats. A fourth guy in back wore a knit cap, like Michael Nesmith of the Monkees, and jumped around wildly, rapping non-sequiturs like "shit an' a piss." Nothing was amplified, so the audience was forced to sit very close in order to hear. The vocal parts were slightly out of tune, which created an underlying dissonance that Sid found brilliant. He likened it to Arabic vocalists who are trained to sing between individual notes.

Sid loved the idea of combining classic Irish poetry with the language of the modern black street rappers. He saw the multi-ethnic political statement they were making by drawing on the obvious connections between the oppression of the Irish in Great Britain and the Afro-American in the United States. The musical blend was bewitching, as well; he closed his eyes and imagined rockabilly cats singing Nordic sea shanties to the accompaniment of a sidewalk tarantella. He was excited and exhausted by his discovery. After the show, Sid raced backstage and signed the band to a six-figure deal.

They never used instruments again.

Send me back home, oh send me back home.
My time is up and there's nowhere to roam.
I been singin' for years and I can't catch a break.
I feel like St. Patrick and I live like the snakes.
I feel like St. Patrick and I live like the snakes.

The Quest

I called Sorina from the plane. Austin had been strange, somewhat depressing, and I needed to hear her voice, to ground me. I told her about J.D. and what I'd seen, and to return the subject to her attention, added, "I hope all is well with the Quest."

"The Quest sucks," she said.

"And I was hoping you'd cheer ME up," I laughed. "Don't worry, baby, you know I've seen that movie . . . and it's gonna be so nice to take a break together."

The static just about cut us off.

"I'm so burnt . . . who knows," I added, "Austin may have been my last gig."

"Well I've seen THAT movie before, too," she said, knowingly. "You'll die with a guitar in your hands."

"Maybe, but I'd rather die in bed."

"Me, too."

"See you soon."

The Quest is a daily thing; it's a long distance race, you know, not a sprint, which was one of the verbal salves I'd apply to almost any situation as I ventured into the world of the arts. As a child, I was always curious, relatively happy, but never satisfied. I grew up and became easily bored, somewhat happy, and still, never satisfied. The arts beckoned because with the arts, the search is eternal, and that carries certain baggage, on both sides of the scale. It's exciting and daunting, it's rewarding and frustrating, and ultimately, no matter what you accomplish, with the art itself or the public's perception, you're continually challenged and of course, never satisfied. My choice of canvas was music, my tools the guitar, the studio, the timbre of my voice. I joined with souls who had similar, though ever-shifting, de-sires, and we formed a band. And the beast was let loose.

Looking back, I see moments along the way standing out like buoys on a turbulent ocean, popping up with color when all around is stormy gray. One particular moment in mind falls between happy accident and fated destiny, de-pending on how you figure a higher power does or does not play into the Quest.

It was during the height of fall, the air was crisp, the leaves had turned and the sun shone brightly; it was a per-fect day to be outside, bicycling or going on a picnic. So, naturally, we had studio time booked. The song we were working on that day had a sexy tribal groove, if I can be so crude as to describe it that way, and it made your hips move and gyrate in an uncontrollable humping motion. We tried laying the drum tracks down with a full kit, and it translated okay, but ultimately it was still too stiff, metronomic, heavy. It needed to swing, so J.D., our drummer, pulled out his cymbals and snares and tried playing the beat on toms and bass. Some drummers insist on using all their hardware simply because they can—like a writer who flaunts his vo-cabulary. They are technique and flash, but for me, tech-nique is a tool, you have to have soul to know how to use it. J.D. had soul, he had taste, and he was a "songwriter's drummer" and in this case went with a bare bones set-up, which got us closer to manna, but unfortunately didn't quite work either. We thought about laying percussion over what we'd recorded, but at its essence, the track didn't feel quite right and there was no sense in hiding it.

There's a crude studio cliché that goes, "you can't pol-ish a turd." J.D. knew that, too. So, we took a break and went out back for a smoke and stared up at the clear blue sky and pondered the black tar parking lot and finally, no-ticed two old oil drums right next to us, slightly dented and worse for wear, but still begging to be used. I looked at J.D. and he looked at me, and we hauled those suckers into the studio. We tore up a couple of rags and duct taped them around the ends of his sticks, turned the cans upside down. He took a determined look at them as the track began to roll, and then, laid down his part in one take. He sounded like three drummers when he needed to, and one when space beckoned; he constructed and deconstructed, and it all boiled down to our first hit single. When I say hit, I'm exaggerating a bit, but it was the first tune we made any real money on. I cut J.D. in as a co-writer, which some said I shouldn't have, but to me, the groove made the tune; he

painted my ideas perfectly on this effervescent track en-
titled "Upbeat Love Stomp."

> *There's an old joke that goes like this.*
> *Mother to son: "What do you want to be when*
> *   you grow up?"*
> *"A drummer," he replies.*
> *She looks at him, fondly, as only a mother can.*
> *"But, honey," she says, "you can't do both."*

As soon as I saw those drums, my mind flashed back to
my grandmother's house in east Missouri. There were two
large oil drums out back by the alley, rusted brown and
burnt black. After dinner, it was my job to take out the
garbage and burn it, in the days when that sort of thing
was common practice. You could look up and down the
alley around 7, 8 o'clock and see smoke hovering over a
whole series of drums and steel garbage cans, paired in
twos and threes. It smelled like summer with all that garbage burning, but it wasn't a bad smell, it didn't cut with
the kind of pungency you might expect. Every once in a
while, a truck came down the alley, crunching the gravel
under its wheels, passing through clouds of smoke twisting through the air. The gravel kicked up and sometimes
a larger rock would bounce up and hit a can or drum,
ringing clear as a spoon against a glass of water, pitched
just right, a sound that filtered through my ears and sank
into my bones and holed up for years, waiting for the day
it could come out and play.

There were a million sounds in those days, it seems,
floating around and filling the air and all you had to do
was cock your head to one side, lend an ear, and pick
them out. The sounds weren't pre-processed or electri-
fied, they existed as part of the human experience, part
of the balance of the world. Everything from the cicadas
humming in the trees to the crickets chirping beneath the
front porch, and a half-dozen melodious birds I could never
name. Late at night, I could hear them, one group starting after the other, percussive, not in time, but of it, further accentuated by the third group who held back and
covered both in gentle counterpoint. The wind also had a
certain sound all its own and sometimes it'd blow through
the willow by the side of the house and I could hear the
branches step back and forth, move and sway, scratching
up against the siding. For better or worse, I believe music was more organic back then, as a result of all those

sounds. Or maybe it was just the magic of my grandmother's house.

"So, what do you think?" I asked the engineer. "Should we leave it or lay some percussion on?" I was fishing, see, I was really into those clanky Tom Waits records, so much so, that it created this bad habit of me wanting to put kitchen sink percussion on everything. I think I was also trying to put extra focus on J.D. and his talents, ironic considering the way things turned out.

The engineer nodded his head as we listened back. All we had down was J.D.'s oil drums, a stand-up bass and my scratch vocals, but you could tell the groove was there. The melody was implied within the lyrics and the phrasing, and supported by whatever tune the band could help me carry. Something was happening and all was get out of the way. The engineer, normally stone-faced and non-committal to his clients, actually began to smile, which I felt in these circumstances was akin to a standing O at his favorite club.

"The drums sound cool, man," he said slowly. "I wouldn't have thought of doing it that way, but they work." Then he paused, "but of course, it depends on what you're going for."

J.D. had been outside smoking, but as he came in to the dark bowels of the studio, he caught the end of the playback and immediately said he thought the take was happening and I took this as the second opinion I needed. He had confidence in this one, especially considering it was his only run-through.

"Alright," I said. "It's a keeper. No sense beating it to death."

After round tabling a hundred bad titles, we decided to call the CD *Beating It to Death*. We laughed about it at the time, but it was an omen really, a macabre joke that played itself out over the coming years.

We were a Chicago-based band and our first road trip ever was down to St. Louis for a two-night stand at a club on Delmar Avenue, called Caesar's. It was a tiny room, downstairs from a pizza parlor, and located in the vicinity of Washington University. We crossed the Mississippi early on the day of the gig, checked into a Days Inn, bummed around the pool for awhile and then headed down to the club. The area around the club was supposed to be the "hip" part of town, but it was basically a couple of used bookstores, a few bars and restaurants, and a great record shop called

Vintage Vinyl. The gigs went great—both nights there were packed crowds, and since no one knew who we were, we figured the venues must draw naturally and regularly from the college crowd. We didn't have a record out at the time, and we really weren't sure what "going on the road" was going to do for us, career-wise. We didn't care, though, we just wanted to get out there and do it, and playing as much as possible, in as many settings as we could, wherever we could, was part of it.

St. Louis became part of our regular circuit. If you were planning a strategic attack, you'd put a map on the wall, stick a thumbtack in Chicago, tie a piece of string to it, and then make a huge circle. The circle would encompass Michigan (Ann Arbor, Detroit, Grand Rapids), Indiana (Bloomington), downstate Illinois (Champaign), Missouri (St. Louis), Iowa (Iowa City, Ames, Cedar Falls), Minnesota (Minneapolis), and Wisconsin (Madison and Milwaukee). Lots of college towns and "secondary markets." But, people came out, and we got paid decent and we got better.

And so did St. Louis. The area around Caesar's drew more activity, Delmar got more crowded, there were more bookstores, bars and restaurants, and coffee shops. Caesar's moved to a bigger venue across the street, and Vintage Vinyl just got more crowded. The city put in a "walk of fame" proudly honoring all the people with attachments to St. Louis, those who were born there or spent significant time in its clutches. It was impressive, I mean, you had Miles Davis, Chuck Berry, Harry Caray, Ike Turner—a lot of rugged individualists had graced this town.

One night we were down there opening for a national band, I can't even remember who, and after our very short set, I began to get the itch to go outside. The other band were really nice guys and their crew treated us great, but I don't know, we'd been out for about a week and I was already feeling claustrophobic. Since the rest of the band was hanging for the night, it gave me license to escape.

So, I wandered out alone, reading the names on the walk as I meandered my way down the street, past hurried groups of men and women laughing, carefree chatter and drunken staccato flying by like the spinning of the dial on your FM player. I love to tune in to snatches of conversation when I can, they give you great ideas for songs. And there's also something special about those summer nights; it's hot and sticky, but I don't know, a breeze will sweep by now and again and it feels like a cool drink and brings you back to your senses and reminds you that you are in shirtsleeves and things are as they should be, because it's the middle of August and after all, you're in St. Louis, so things are hot and sticky and as they should be.

Finally, I was wakened to reality by the sound of a real heavy bass guitar line, accompanied by a cracking snare hitting distinctly behind the beat. I had come to an open door, there was the Jamaican flag in the window and inside, five Rastafarian guys and a woman bobbed up and down, their instruments close to their bodies as they worked the tiny stage. A guy in shorts and his girlfriend, dressed in tight pedal pusher pants and a tube top, danced in front of the stage, sweating, moving excitedly out of rhythm. A few other folks sat at two tables up front nodding their heads, and there were maybe half a dozen men and women at the bar doing the same. I love reggae music and they sounded like they were on it, so I ventured in. "Three bucks" the doorman said. I dug out a fiver and told him to keep it. I wandered over to the bar and found a seat and sunk in to listen.

I ordered a Red Stripe and found a comfortable seat at the bar, nursing it slowly, soaking up the music. The woman in the band walked up to the microphone said, "here is a song by one of our rock steady favorites, Ken Boothe."

"Whooooo, Ken Boothe, YEAH!" a girl screamed next to me.

It was loud as hell and the bass player smiled as the band launched into the number.

"Why, why baby why, why did you leave me?" the singer sang, plaintively.

I'm a huge Ken Boothe fan. I turned and saw the girl smiling and shaking her fist in the air.

"I *love* Ken Boothe," she said.

"Yeah, me too."

"Now I Know," she said

"Can't You See?" I responded.

Oh yes, definitely.

I couldn't believe it. One doesn't want to profile, but she looked like a farm girl, freckles, hair tightly rubber-banded into a ponytail. Her shirt said "cowboy" across the front, and it went down almost to her midriff, where a quick glance revealed a sparkling navel ring. She was wearing blue jeans, no flares. It might not be too unusual to find a girl like that in a reggae bar, but it would be rare to run across one with such intense knowledge of the great Ken Boothe.

We got to talking. People tend to tell me their life stories when I meet them, particularly out on the road. It reinforces this innate belief I have that we are increasingly a world of disconnected people trying to make connections. Either that or I just look like a good listener. She was a premed student, studied biology at Washington U, and now was at school in Columbia, U of Missouri. She was visiting family in St. Louis, her mother and stepsisters. Her father was a musician, he left the mom, classic story, and was down in Texas now somewhere with his guitar and his songs, and it sounded like he wasn't exactly successful. She was torn, because on one hand she was very into science, and the idea of helping people through medicine, and was very methodical in her thinking. On the other hand, she had a wild side, she said; she would have tons of piercings and tattoos and would dye her hair blue if anyone would hire her looking like that. She felt like she was a creative soul, but she had nothing to create with. I told her anything could be creative—the best doctors are artists, I said. She smiled. Her name was Sorina. Sorina Johnson. Strange combination. But so was she, a juxtaposition of styles. She gave me information in pieces, as if she was a child with a handful of balloons, hesitant to pass them out.

Finally, she asked what I did, and I told her we'd just played that night. I told her we get to St. Louis and Columbia fairly often and I'd like to stay in touch. I liked her, but I wasn't at the point where I wanted to have some one-night stand, and that was all I could see happening at the time. She wrote her number on the back of a cardboard coaster and I tore it in half and did the same. I finished my beer and reached over to give her a hug and she told me she had a good time. As I left the bar, I felt like we'd been on a date already, like I had just dropped her off at home, only home was a barstool at the reggae bar. Where were her friends, anyway?

Meanwhile, the band kept gigging and *Beating It to Death* was actually a bit of a hit for us, in the sense it got us a good amount of real AAA airplay on many Channel One radio stations and markedly raised our visibility. Those guys at CO are like Satan at the Gates of Hell and I think the label put something like $75,000 into promotions, which was just unheard of at the time for a band at our level of experience. It would all come out of our pockets eventually, but we were hungry and felt ready, if not to conquer the world, well, at least to conquer America. Or the Midwest. We should have figured out how to conquer ourselves, first, but that's another story.

Now, as I mentioned, this first "hit" I've been telling you about, as well several other songs on the record, listed J.D. and myself as co-writers. As a result, I'd say this CD brought J.D. more attention than ever before, from both our own circle of friends and outside world/media at large. Not coincidentally, he began pushing to take the oil drums on the road with us and recasting the bulk of our material, old and new, to conform to the oil drum approach. The other guys in the band balked and so did I. The drums were a good idea *on certain tunes*, but I didn't want to be typecast as some sort of novelty band. Bobby, our guitarist, played electric banjo through a wah-wah pedal on one cut, but that didn't mean we were going to put electric banjo on everything; it would have been ridiculous. Besides, songs are like children in that they often grow up to be what they want to be—they suggest a certain arrangement the way people suggest a certain suit of clothes.

Although Bobby, Mo, and myself all felt strongly about this, J.D. persevered and somehow we wound up taking the oil drums on tour. We were able to draw the line on some material and I guess in retrospect, we thought we were compromising for the good of the whole, but the truth is, the result threw the whole presentation into imbalance, the compromise simply presenting us as a sort of lowest common denominator musical experience.

This was also a turning point for J.D., as he begun to slide down the slope of lost perspective. It's easier than you think, to get thrown off track after plugging away for years, taking shit the whole time for doing this one particular thing, and then all of a sudden waking up to a world that praises you for doing the very same thing. If you're part of a band, and you do get singled out, you might start believing that you are the star of the show and lose sight of your place in the whole.

J.D. also had one of those classic addictive personalities. In our early days, it was relatively innocent—picking up a hobby a week, from drying fresh fruit into strips to playing Ker-Plunk all night. Like anyone, he'd have a beer or two during or after the gig, and that seemed to increase, but not in a damaging sense; from what we could tell it didn't affect his playing or his personality in any negative way. He was what's known as a "happy drunk."

Then as the road trips got longer, J.D. insisted on doing as much driving as he could, and became fiercely protective of the wheel. He wouldn't even let us hire a driver when we were able. We began calling him "Captain D," after the fast-food restaurant or the pillar of death, depending on where we were headed and how fast we were going. He'd get in this groove where he'd take uppers all night to stay awake and become so wired that by morning he could barely see the highway or anything on it. So, he had to sleep then, and in order to do it, he'd crash on a handful of downers, putting on a blindfold and wrapping himself up in a blanket or sleeping bag in the back of the van. J.D. would stay knocked out all day, right up until sound check, and when he awoke, sweaty and disoriented, it wasn't in the guise of a happy pill-taker.

One of the worst incidents happened when we did a midnight show at GB VII in New York. We went into the club for sound check about seven o'clock and returned to the van about twenty minutes later to get something from Bobby's tool kit, only to find that the lock on the driver's door was jammed. We entered from the passenger's side and sure enough, his tools were gone, along with a PA mixer, some smelly shirts we'd hung on hooks in the back, and J.D.'s backpack, which happened to be filled with irreplaceable tapes from his days as a college d.j. We should have known better; this was the East Village in Manhattan, back in the day, right off the Bowery, a rough and ominously deserted save for crack addicts and winos. The stuff was probably up on Columbus Circle by dawn the next day, laid out on blankets for sale by loud and steady hucksters. Don't know, I guess we were so full of ourselves and our mission, common sense was often the last thing we packed

Anyway, J.D. was so wired on pills, I thought he was going to kill one of us, but we stood by silently as his anger shifted and became re-directed at the anonymous inhabitants of what was appropriately called, for J.D.'s sake, the city that never sleeps. Slowly, he began stalking the alleyways of the East Village like a mad vigilante. He found a broken baseball bat lying in the middle of the street and began waving it menacingly, threatening to "kill the nigger" who stole his backpack. It was an ugly sight—I had never heard J.D. use the 'n' word before and believed him to be incapable of such a thing. He may have been saying it just to piss us off, to get a reaction, but as I looked up and down the dimly lit, visibly deserted city block, I feared for him and ourselves. I feared for something beyond the obvious immediate dangers, something murkier and less defined, and more connected to what we were doing as a band, sacrifices we were making to what end. As ridiculous as it may sound, the only comparison I can think of is being stuck in a marriage you know isn't going to work, but you feel obligated to keep trying, because you've grown so accustomed to each other, that you would miss the pain. We followed J.D. through those darkened streets and as showtime approached, we had the excuse we needed to gently tow him back into the relative safety of the club.

> *There's another familiar joke that goes something like this.*
> *"What do you call a guy who likes to hang around musicians?"*
> *Answer: a drummer.*
> *Insert canned laughter.*
> *It's all about context, though, isn't it?*

I must admit, J.D. was a great drummer, and as anyone knows, a great drummer drives a rock and roll band—the motor and the foundation.

After New York, my brother copied me on an e-mail he received from my aunt. She asked if I enjoyed playing all those gigs. Then, before he could answer, she added, "Oh yes, he must, that's what he wants to do someday." I don't know which was more depressing, my aunt tossing off my life's work in a sentence or my brother cc-ing me on the e-mail. I'm not saying this to be dramatic, but sometimes I think I'm too sensitive for this world.

I spoke with Sorina regularly on the phone, long conversations, often late at night. We had a lot in common and I enjoyed our talks, though typically, she moved from being very warm and flirtatious to a distance that seemed self-imposed. The next time the band hit St. Louis, we scheduled a dinner date, after sound check and before the show. We had a lovely time, as we shared our stories of the moment, the pressures of med school and all it entailed for her, and my latest ups and downs with J.D., and life in the world of the Quest, as I liked to call it. She liked that and began to use it herself, when speaking of her goals and ambitions. She couldn't make our gig, as she had to get back to Columbia, but I was okay with that. Glad, even. We kissed for the first time that night, after I walked her to her car. The kiss lingered longer than most, and her lips felt warm and comfortable. She pulled away, but smiled, and reassured me that she had had a nice time.

Somehow, the band made it through all connected to *Beating It to Death*, oil drums included. The disc had decent sales and airplay and it was moving us along, but it became clear it wasn't going to break us—that would be up to the next release—if we were lucky. A logical move would've been to improve upon all the key elements that got us there in the first place, the great group interplay, good accessible (yet not lightweight) tunes, and both solid and quirky rhythm glue. We had a very hot indie producer lined up to work the next project, and we were all ready to turn it up a notch, as the expression goes. I should qualify that—when I say all of us, I'm excluding J.D.

This marked the beginning of J.D.'s "rock star" phase, which in my opinion, sadly belied our relatively fringe status. Unlike his erratic but dependable tour behavior, J.D. began showing up late for recording sessions, often sloppy drunk, sometimes too tanked to play. Other times, he was just plain strange. Once he came to the studio dressed as an ice cream man, with a cooler under his arm, and spent the whole night sitting on the floor by his drums, eating Eskimo Pies, one by one. Another time, he was about four hours late because he refused to miss his high school buddies' annual Halloween party. We worked on vocals that night, on tracks we'd already finished and when he finally showed up dressed as Fred Flintstone, we let him collapse in the corner with paper mache club in hand. Bobby had a talk with him after that and he became coherent for a time, at which point we began hurrying to get his parts down before he wigged out again. Finally, as if to throw us another loop, he insisted that all he would ever play again were the oil drums—on each and every song. Rather than argue, we agreed and cut them to a click track, thinking we could hire someone else to put real drums on later. That's how bad things had become.

Now, if this wasn't enough, Morris, our bass player, began having personal problems. His dad had been fighting cancer for a couple of years, but chemotherapy wasn't working anymore and the end was rapidly approaching. Morris was having a hard time getting through the sessions, and while we hoped and prayed for the best for all involved, we were hoping the death watch would go long enough so that he could finish his parts. Ironically, Mo's dad, a former musician, pushed him the hardest, encouraging Morris to spend less time at the hospital and more in the studio. I think he thought great things were about to happen for his son's band.

Nevertheless, Morris struggled, and about mid-way through the record, "caused" another incident I'll never forget. This time J.D. was actually present and coherent and we had set up our gear and began checking levels when we realized something was amiss. Morris wasn't there, and he was a man who was never known to be late for anything, his punctuality and good breeding as much a part of him as the perfectly styled hair swept back across his forehead. We silently speculated amongst ourselves as to the reason for his delay, hoping for the best and skirting the obvious out of superstition, save for J.D., who began pacing, mumbling and cursing. "I've got cancer, too, you know . . . I'm dying of cancer, too." J.D. repeated this over and over as he spun around the studio, directing the words at me, the engineer, Bobby, and a couple of techs who stuck their heads into the booth in the midst of the chaos. "I'm dying of cancer too, where the fuck is he? I'm dying of cancer . . ." J.D.'s speech continued dark and clipped in the controlled ambiance of the studio, hitting hard against the dull padded walls that surrounded us. The room filled quickly with the worst of vibes, a thick tension incompatible with the whole creative process, ironic considering we had planned to start with the basics for "Love Thy Brother," a somewhat tongue-in-cheek ska song about tolerance and acceptance.

When Morris finally made it, only fifty past the hour (maybe twenty minutes late in real time), he looked as tired and haggard as I'd ever seen him. A diminutive strong man, Morris was the gentle soul of the band, a class act who immediately *apologized* for spending so much time with his dying father. He opened his case and slung on his bass, looking forlorn and sad as he bent over his tuner and peered into the LED lights with hazy red eyes. His hair was unusually tousled and his shirt was wrinkled and stained, with giant half moons of sweat under the arms, odd considering he was the only guy in the band who took an iron on the road. Actually, I think he was the only one of us who even *owned* an iron. Bobby cracked open a beer and set it on Morris's amp as he tuned. Morris whispered a "thank you." I patted him on the shoulder and walked over to pick up my guitar, strapping it on in silence. We were trying to clear up the fog and start over, back to the beginning of our musical lives, when we were locked in with a collective joy that would be impossible for me to describe here, other than saying it was our reason for being, a something special aura that could rid a room of all its demons. But, sad to say, as soon as J.D. came out of the bathroom and saw Mo standing there, we knew the night was doomed. His eyes bugged out exaggeratedly, as he slowly approached Morris from behind, whispering in a low, steadily rising voice, "Where were you, mannn? I've got cancer, too, you know."

Morris picked up the beer bottle and emptied it over J.D.'s head, suds cascading majestically down the length of his dirty blonde hair. J.D. was stunned, but before he could react, Morris reached out one hand like an officer stopping traffic, toppling him backwards and more importantly, removing him from his personal space. Mo watched him fall and then stormed outside. We couldn't blame him, really. "Love Thy Brother" never made the record.

We worked long and hard on *Pounding the Pavement*, the working title for that CD, and despite all our conflicts—or perhaps because of it, we all managed to agree on one thing. It was a great piece of work. In fact, I still listen to the rough mixes, and I don't do that with any of my past efforts. However, the man who had signed us at the label had since been fired and his replacement did not share our enthusiasm. The label kept pushing the release date back, a few months at a time, until after about a year, they finally informed us that they were dropping us altogether. Since they paid for the recording and owned the master to this one, it'd probably never see the light of day.

> And you must remember, it's all about context.
> "What do you call a drummer without a girlfriend?"
> Answer: homeless.

Naturally, the Quest took a different shape when we were dropped. On the one hand, it was sobering and depressing, all the time and energy spent building this something that had suddenly vanished into nothing. On the other hand, like anything in life, when one door closes, another will open, and new opportunities arise. I was conflicted, though, between optimism and realism. I was also conflicted between continuing with Sorina and cutting things off before they got too serious. We were spending more time together, as schedules permitted, shuttling back for quick weekends, occasionally she meeting up with me at third-point destinations on the road.

We had always been close, it seemed, but now our intimacy had reached new depths and along with the shakiness of the band, I was contemplating whether or not this was the logical conclusion to one phase of my life, or the beginning of another. I was like that guy in the movies, the old slapstick numbers, who has one foot on the dock and another on the boat and the boat begins to drift and his feet start to widen and he can't decide whether to jump back on the dock, or over on the boat. His indecision gets the best of him, and he finally falls into the water with a splash.

The week we were dropped, I called Sorina to see what her schedule was like and we were able to hook up in St. Louis for a four-day stretch. I remember being pretty quiet and withdrawn when I arrived, but she pulled me out of it over a nice Italian dinner down by the river. Afterwards we went back to our hotel room and took a long hot bath together and talked about everything in both of our lives and between us. After that, we slipped into silence. And then we slipped into bed. And then we poured out our anxieties through long slow deliberate motions. And she never pulled away again.

As she nestled into me in the darkness of the hotel room, one leg wrapped around my body, her touch was the only sensation I felt. In those days, the darkness of my hotel room at night used to surround me and comfort me, the only constant in an ever changing world. A publicity person once told me my name means "gray murky sea" in Latin.

What do you call a drummer in a suit?
The defendant!

I felt as if J.D. was standing trial for the world the last time I saw him onstage. It was two years after the band split up. I was down in Austin doing a solo gig at a big well-known music festival, where lots of bands and musicians from around the country go to play for free in the hopes of furthering their careers via contacts or exposure. Some do. Most don't. Regardless, the people running the conference, the clubs, the radio promoters, the publicity agents, the hotels, the record labels, and just about anyone else involved, profit handsomely. This is the corporate entity rock and roll has become, and I often wonder whether old-school pioneers like Robert Johnson and Charley Patton would have participated in such events, had they existed in their day. We'll never know. My guess is "no."

Anyway, at the time I was just finishing my first solo record and looking for someone to put it out. I thought it would be good to go down to Austin, do a show, and let people know what I was up to. And so I did. After the show,

I found myself wandering past yet another strip of bars and restaurants, this time it was Sixth Street, dodging sailors on leave and winding around an endless stream of fraternity boys and sorority girls out for the night, aimlessly poking my head into a bar now and again for five minutes of music. The strip was relatively free of music executives— they were all in their hotels watching the NCAA basketball championhips on T.V., earning their tax write-offs for "scouting" bands. Along the way, I was surprised to see a well-lit neon sign next to the entrance of Joe's Rock Club, advertising Jumping Jack Flash and his Pavement Pounders. J.D.s real name was Jonas Brazinski, and sometimes he liked to call himself Jack Flash. As I read the sign, I immediately knew at least two of the songs he'd be performing.

I walked in and I was even more surprised to find the club somewhat crowded. Most of the patrons were wearing laminates around their neck, meaning they were industry types, attendees from the fest. I figured they were baseball fans, as well. I ordered a Coke from the bartender and found an empty table near the back of the room where a high window looks out on the crowded street. Outside, the masses moved back and forth, occasionally brushing the glass like the ocean at high tide. Through the dim lights of the club, I saw the stage set-up was obviously designed to focus on J.D. There was a boom stand with microphone up front, a stool, and three large oil drums, cords and mikes protruding like the arms of an octopus. A bass rig was positioned to the right, and a battered upright piano to the left, it looked like cherry wood to me. I nursed my Coke, chewed on an ice cube and waited. The room filled up some more, and finally, the stage lights came on. A large fat man with a black Harley t-shirt came on and gave a lengthy introduction, greatly exaggerating the accomplishments of our band and J.D. as a solo artist. During this spiel, the bassist and piano player took their positions. Would you please welcome, he asked, and everyone responded, scattered but enthusiastic applause for my old friend Jonas Brazinski.

A curtain opened at the back of the stage and two hefty bouncers emerged, holding J.D. upright with his legs suspended in the sitting position, as if he had been lifted right off the toilet. His arms were draped around their shoulders as they hauled him across the stage and brought him to the stool in the center of the stage. J.D. smiled a tiny woozy smile when they set him down, like he was thoroughly enjoying himself but lacked the energy for further expression. Everything about him seemed smaller than it should be—even his hair, while long, seemed brittle and prematurely aged, falling like broken icicles around his shoulders. I had heard through the grapevine about his M.S., but his frame seemed terribly withered and thin and it was sad for me to see that his legs weren't even functional. For a moment, I wondered how he was even going to play, but then, I remembered, musically J.D. had always been game for anything. The two men positioned him further on the stool, wrapping each foot and ankle around the rung of the barstool, to help fix him in place. J.D. pointed to the floor, after which one man picked up a bottle of whiskey sitting there, unscrewed the cap and handed it to J.D., who took a very long swig. He smiled again, this one directed at the audience, and set the bottle down on the drum in front of him. Then he picked up two large club-like sticks, exaggerated in appearance by his spidery hands, half-turned over his shoulder to the bassist and shouted the count, leading with a short roll on the four. The band picked it up and slid into "Upbeat Love Stomp," as J.D. and the bassist locked into a familiar groove. His whiskey bottle fell to the floor with a crash and one of the bouncers hurried to the bar for another. The rhythm section was smooth and syncopated, holding on tight while the piano player dropped a series of jazz runs in and around the beat, a nice addition to the original arrangement. We had been strictly a guitar band.

The song's finish was greeted with scattered but enthusiastic applause and J.D. nodded in acknowledgment, as the bass player kicked into the lead-off riff of "Pounding the Pavement." I scouted the crowd and saw at least a few well-dressed types nodding in appreciation, looking good, but out of time. J.D. righted himself and grimaced slightly partway through the first chorus, something most in the audience probably didn't notice. But I did. His drumming was solid, but it lagged in this song. It looked to me as if he was having trouble gripping his sticks. Somehow, the band pushed him through it, but as I sat and watched, I saw each song leading J.D. further down the steps of debilitation, musically and otherwise. After the hits, the material grew thinner, with some weak new stuff and even a couple of terribly lame cover tunes. The set ended with a reprise of "Upbeat Love Stomp," after which the bouncers came back and carried J.D. off, as he waved over his shoulder to the crowd. About a quarter of the club was empty now, but those remaining were satisfied—in a sense, J.D. had always been a consummate showman and he certainly gave his fans what they wanted. The band's disintegration and split had been messy, but in my heart, I wanted to let bygones be bygones and go backstage for a congratulatory greeting. But I didn't budge from my stool.

The next morning I checked out of my hotel and hopped a plane back home, which was about to be St. Louis. Sorina had begun a residency and we were going to share an apartment together. A single bead of sweat ran down the side of my face, so I reached up to turn up the little round fan above my head, to cool me down. I was nervous. I was never afraid of flying, but I was afraid of what I might do when I landed, that's exactly what J.D. found so difficult. I thought of him as I stared into the bright blue sky that remains suspended for all time above endless waves of clouds, outside endless airplane windows, to cover me between an endless string of unclaimed destinations. After the plane landed, I grabbed my bag from the overhead compartment and walked down the long tunnel, white light growing nearer, just like one of those late night television testimonials on near-death experiences. At the very end, the light made a splash, the space opened wide and it wasn't Jesus, but wonderful noise and people, staccato bursts, and sounds that could be stories. I passed a gathering of people holding flowers and signs, and I thought about writing a song about people waiting for people at airports. Then I saw Sorina standing in front of me, leaning one hand against a pole, waiting for me, and I thought how, that too, would make a good song. She jumped up and hugged me, tightly, without reservation.

"And how was the Quest?" she asked.

And not for a moment did I think about my gig in Austin, the sadness of J.D.'s performance, highs and lows of past shows, or future challenges. No, the minute I saw Sorina all I could think of was she and I together, the commitment, and a strange combination of fear and wild yet desperate exhilaration.

"I'd say the Quest has just begun."

"Really? I thought you were going to quit," she said, goading me.

"Never. You know that when I'm in something I'm in it for good."

"Oh really?" she said, smiling.

"Of course," I responded with exaggerated confidence. "And you?" We were booking through the airport and I was hurrying to keep up with her, though her strides were considerably shorter. "When I called from the plane, you said it sucked."

"Oh, I was just messing with you," she answered, grabbing my duffel bag from one hand so I was free to use the shoulder strap on my guitar. "I mean, the residency is gonna be a bitch, but it's a good challenge, you know, and anyway, as of right now," she stopped, pausing, completely in time, "theQuest is over."

I stopped cold before the automatic doors.

"Come on," she said, forging ahead, motioning.

I'd always had a hard time living life not expecting the worst. "What do you mean," I asked, reading all sorts of disaster into her words.

"For me," she continued, as we headed into the parking lot, "the Quest ended in a little reggae bar on Delmar Avenue, so many nights ago."

More poetry than I'd ever mastered in one of my songs, she was always right, and it made me sick sometimes. It also made me realize that nothing was ever in vain, that no matter where things were headed, or where they are headed, the Quest was all one, it wove together incrementally and magically pushed me into places I never would have gone. It was both a beginning and an end. And one followed the other. And as we loaded our luggage into our car, readying ourselves for the drive to our new home, I thanked all there was for the Quest.

Portugal

Sean dressed that morning in clothes that ordinarily remained untouched in the furthest corners of his closet. The black pleated slacks and dull granite sports jacket were thrift store specials he'd stumbled across in Davenport, Iowa, the Italian shoes were ordered on eBay, and the collarless shirt was the result of a half hour's worth of haggling with a cheery Pakistani shopkeeper in London, on a rainy day, seemingly a million years ago. In reality, it had only been thirteen months.

Sean had no idea how it happened, but somewhere in that short space of time, a strong wind blew and to the ground bent the row of endless possibilities at his disposal, and when they snapped back again, well, they didn't snap back, but remained bent into variations of the lessers of many evils. But, he knew that life was more or less a big spin of the roulette wheel where one fought to survive, drew soul from the victories, and tried to make the world a better place then when you left it. That's all anyone could do.

He flipped on satellite and drove through the downtown and out onto the interstate, his mind wandering onto mental images of slaves who built the pyramids by carrying the wealth of the pharaohs on their backs, serfs that toiled and sweated over the fields of monarchs for centuries, and African noblemen who were sold, sometimes by their own brothers, to be shipped to America where they built great cities across the country. These were dark thoughts for the morning of an interview, but he couldn't help himself. Then Billie Holiday came on the radio singing a Cole Porter song and his spirits were instantly lifted. The sun replaced the rain clouds that had hung over the city and he spotted a rainbow peeking over the hill as he exited and drove upwards into Maryland Farms Business Park. He thought about his girlfriend safe at home with their twins, a boy and a girl, both learning to smile and cry simultaneously, readying for a world that was blindingly beautiful and terrifically evil.

Sean parked in an open space directly in front of Suite 202, checked the fine print on the door to make sure he was in the right place, and entered. A blonde receptionist who was sunnier than the day outside could ever be told him to wait; Mr. Rightly would be right with him. She asked if he wanted something to drink and gave him some choices.

"A pop sounds good," he answered, measuring her strange look as she disappeared into the back and reemerged with a cold Pepsi.

"Here's your Coke," she said, "and can you please sign our in/out book when you get a chance?" Each word rose in pitch, to underscore her cheer.

Sean did as she asked and sat down in a little black leather chair with silver metal arms in the opposite corner of the waiting area, perpendicular to a plastic plant on a glass table and another little black leather chair with silver metal arms. He opened up the leather-covered day planner his girlfriend had suggested he bring to the interview to make himself look more professional. Inside, there were pages of background on the company, facts, figures, and historical information he'd printed out from their website.

Sean's girlfriend also recommended that he think of the interview like a first date, where both parties decide if they like each other and whether they want to continue with their relationship. He couldn't ever remember doing research on a girl before going out on a first date, although at times it probably would have been a good idea. The way *he* looked at the interview, it was like working an audience, and an audience of one was always the easiest to win over because they weren't influenced by those around them. And so he read the coffee-stained copy he'd printed from the website, learned about the history of Rightly Drink Caddies, as well as their other party favors, memorized where Mr. Rightly went to school, browsed through some adobe newsletters and thought, shit, I can write circles around these guys.

University of Nebraska, University of Nebraska, University of Nebraska, Sean repeated over and over to himself like a mantra, before writing it on the palm of his left hand with a Sharpie. He'd always hated over-rehearsing, preferring to leave something for the show, and so he put his papers away and busied himself watching the receptionist tap away on her computer, punctuating the sound of the hits of the sixties and seventies station that filled the room. The blinds were closed, but sunlight crept through the cracks in finely drawn lines. Finally, a muffled voice came over the speaker phone, and the receptionist stood up.

"Mr. Rightly is ready."

Sean followed her down a newly carpeted hallway, the smell of fresh paint filling his nostrils, until he turned right and entered Mr. Rightly's office, where the scent was replaced by the fresh smell of Krispy Kreme donuts. Sure enough there was a box open on the desk, and his first vision of Mr. Rightly was that of a tall red-haired man wiping chocolate icing off his lips, flakes of the sugary stuff falling onto his desk like snow in the Catskills.

"These donuts are delicious," Mr. Rightly said, for a greeting. He stepped from around the desk to shake hands and Sean noticed they were about the same height. "Please sit down," Mr. Rightly said, politely gesturing to another empty black and silver chair, which sat opposite his brown imitation oak desk.

"Tell me about yourself," he began.

"I see, yes, yes, yes," he muttered as Sean answered.

"Where did you go to college?" he continued.

Mr. Rightly apparently hadn't read Sean's resume very closely, but that was a plus, because it was very thin. The academic credentials were stellar, but there was a gap in his work experience, a gap where he had left the office, presumably, for good. Mr. Rightly delivered all the questions very deliberately, which unsettled Sean and caused him to pause before answering.

"Would you consider yourself a team player?" he added.

Sean didn't feel good about how things were going.

"Do you work well under deadline?" he said, with emphasis on the word deadline.

The wall behind Mr. Rightly was covered with travel posters of Portugal. Sean had done a gig there once, a festival in a beautiful open field, with skies of blue and the smell of water coming in over the ocean, washing everyone down like love personified. In fact, it was so great, he made sure he never played Portugal again because he knew it couldn't have been repeated. Funny thing about traveling, he'd had so many wonderful experiences in so many places, but it always left him a little melancholy, like you couldn't simply live everywhere at once, nor could you live more than one life. Sometimes he wondered if musicians simply left a little piece of themselves everywhere they went, until eventually, they vanished into thin air.

Sean asked Mr. Rightly if he liked it there, pointing his finger at the happy people in the poster. Rightly swiveled halfway around in his chair and spent what seemed a long time surveying the beautiful boy and girl laughing their cares away.

"I don't know, I've never been," he finally said, before chortling aloud, his bulbous nose lighting up like a firefly. "I couldn't think of anything else to put up, so my secretary suggested it. She has a friend who's a travel agent."

The phone was ringing down the hall, but otherwise the offices were silent, so much so, Sean could hear delivery trucks zoom by on the road outside the parking lot, carrying packages to some unknown destination, places of excitement, like New York, Amsterdam, Portugal even, places he'd been to and may never return.

"So," Mr. Rightly said, dusting some donut crumbs off the resume in front of him, "I see you've done different kinds of writing, but tell me, how would you effectively write about drink caddies?"

Sean's patience was wearing thin, but nevertheless, he answered politely and enthusiastically, as he spoke of how written communication was sadly becoming a lost art in the world we lived in. Words mattered, and if you convey the correct message about your drink caddies, he told Mr. Rightly, it will mean everything in the company's future success.

"All my writing carries both emotion and precision," he said, definitively. It was one of the few truthful moments of the interview, for Sean.

Mr. Rightly nodded, seemingly impressed. His eyes returned to the resume.

"Where do you see yourself in five years?"

"Portugal," Sean blurted out.

Mr. Rightly reached for another donut and Sean groaned inside, knowing his newfound discipline and preparation had failed him. He put his hand on his forehead, to hide his eyes from conveying either sarcasm or satire to the red-haired man. He saw the words "University of Nebraska" etched there in black marker. "Stupid, stupid, stupid," he thought to himself, rubbing his hands together to remove the crib note.

When Sean looked up again, Mr. Rightly was standing, towering over him. The drink caddie heir swallowed and mumbled something about being in contact.

Driving back down the hill, all Sean could think about was the serfs and the pharoahs. Or was it the kings and the slaves? He felt depressed, and yet relieved. It was almost as if being asked to interview was more important to him than actually getting the job, it somehow validated a need to succeed in their world as well as his own. Or, maybe he was afraid of succeeding more in their world than his own. He flipped on the radio this time, and hit some buttons and pretty soon it was Marvin Gaye and Tammi Terrell, so beautiful together, singing "Ain't No Mountain High Enough."

When he pulled up to the house, the song was over, and his girlfriend was waiting at the door. She held her cheek out for him to kiss, and smiled broadly.

"It must have gone well," she said, calmly.

"Uh, well, yes, it went okay."

"Better than okay," she said. "Rightly Drink Caddies called to say they want to offer you the job!" She laughed.

"You're kidding?" he asked, incredulous.

"No, they want you to call back as soon as you can, to discuss salary! Well done!"

Sean was too dazed to say anything, and tripped a little on the doorjamb as he followed her back into the house. She turned and threw her arms around his neck. "I bet it was the day planner," she laughed.

"I bet it was," he said, as visions of Portugal rolled forth from his memory like a tidal wave. "I bet it was."

Berlin (a memoir)

In my hometown, we used to go to Dunkin' Donuts late at night, because nothing else was open. My friend and I would talk into the wee hours, about life, love, and politics, over coffee and jelly donuts, our fingers covered with sugar as we bit into the gooey strawberry fillings. We'd sit there and talk about how our lives were going to change once we got out of high school and out of that town and into a world where we could do what we wanted to do. And, because we were young, nothing kept us awake at night.

One time we were talking about John F. Kennedy and the only other customer in the place, swiveling on a stool at the other end of the counter, overheard us and started quoting from a speech Kennedy made in West Berlin back in 1963. Kennedy told an adoring crowd that "All free men, wherever they may live, are citizens of Berlin, and therefore, as a free man, I take pride in the words, *Iche bin ein Berliner*." Kennedy was saying he stood with the Berliners in their struggles to reunite their city and their country, and not surprisingly, they ate it up, no pun intended. From his words, however, an urban legend took root. Since many Germans leave off the "ein" in statements of citizenship, it has been said that Kennedy actually told the crowd that he was a Berliner, or "jelly doughnut."

It's funny how urban legends take hold when you travel to distant places where people have different customs and language. It's also amazing how much can be communicated, despite the shaky translations, because in the end, there is so much of the human experience that is the same. Wherever you are on the globe, there are people following flights of fancy or grounded deliberation, in efforts to cultivate a good life, and in the process, hold on to whatever it takes to get them through the day. I believe most people want the same things out of this crap shoot, they want good health and peace of mind and a safe place where they can wake up every day with someone who loves them and who gives them the opportunity to love back. I also believe most people have a good sense of when someone is being straight with them—in this case, enough sense to know that the President of the United States wouldn't come all that way to tell them he was a jelly doughnut.

As for myself, I got out of the little town and into the world and do at least some of what I've wanted to do. As a traveling troubadour, I've been lucky enough to visit some of the world's greatest cities, setting out on a string of adventures, during which I promote my well-reviewed, poorly selling recorded works of songcraft. When people ask me to speak of my favorite place or places, it's very hard to choose, because they've all been great in one way or another. But, I distinctly remember my first trip to Berlin, where I found myself careening through a landscape populated by a series of memorable urban legends.

Getting to Berlin—Friday, January 24, 2003

The "German tour," as I've labeled it, takes me, due to low budget travel, from Chicago to Amsterdam to Berlin. Then, after I play in Berlin, I travel down to Saxony for a string of shows, double back to Berlin, and return to the Netherlands for a few more gigs before flying back to the States. So, if you can follow this, the morning of my first day in Berlin actually finds me waking up on the plane to Amsterdam, shaken out of sleep by the sound of chattering voices and clinking glasses. I take off my eyeshades and spot a stewardess coming up the aisle, pushing a stainless steel breakfast cart. Bleary eyed passengers with rumpled sweaters and matted hair are standing in line for the toilet, rubbing their faces and shaking their limbs. Before long, we have landed, and I begin the long walk over moving sidewalks and descending escalators, guitar and backpack in hand. Customs is a breeze, as it usually is in the Netherlands, at least partly because of my surname.

"Hoekstra, hmmm," the clerk with the captain's hat says. "Do you know any Dutch?"

"Sorry, no."

"'Tis a pity," he smiles.

I've since learned *Bedankt*. Thank you.

Next to customs, there's the baggage area. Crowds of people are milling about among the conveyer belts and metal chutes, waiting for their belongings to be hurled down the latter and delivered from the former. It's a large room, with artificial light washing several stations of carousels and, truthfully, I could be anywhere, except for the fact that the folks appear to be native Europeans. I say this because they look like people coming home, as opposed to people leaving home—something about the sense of completion, a collective exhale that fills the air like little clouds of invisible cigarette smoke. And, while I detest stereotypes, there are definitely more folks dressed in black, more mixed-race couples, and more people who are carrying low percentages of body fat. Every time I'm in Europe, I really notice how overweight, as a people, Americans are. And, while I grew up with my mother telling me how I always looked like "skin and bones," I find myself fitting right in across the pond. Indeed, I'm usually pegged as a Brit, and I think it's largely because of this.

I spot my luggage, grab it with a heave-ho, go to the round currency exchange hut in the center of the great room and exchange my dollars for euros, call my wife and son, and head off to buy my train ticket. The heart of Schiphol airport is full of polished chrome and clear glass, nondescript save for the giant Styrofoam pieces of Gouda cheese that stand in front of the shops, offering tourists one last chance to bring a piece of the Netherlands home with them, to spread on cheeseburgers and sandwiches. Many tongues of conversation drift past me as I walk from the ticket window downstairs to the train platform, balancing adeptly on the escalator with rolling suitcase, guitar, and backpack in hand and shoulders.

Soon I am aboard a sleek coach resplendent with carpeted floor, doors that glide open and closed at the front and back of each car with the quiet whoosh of compressed air. It is a six and a half hour journey from Amsterdam to Berlin, and we are headed due east, away from the North Sea and towards flat plains, farmland, and grey winter skies. I fall in and out of short dreamless naps, stare out the window, and read from a gripping book my wife recommended I pack for my journey. Eventually I see the train slowing to a stop that reads Hannover, which means we are entering Germany. I think of the last time I was in the country, albeit very shortly, two years before. I was traveling to a show in Limburg, in the corner of the Netherlands, when I took a wrong turn and accidentally crossed the German border. My tour guide, a native Dutchman, spotted a German truck and bitterly joked, "They are bringing our bicycles back."

Dusk is falling, but the landscape hasn't changed, I see rows of fallow brown farmland stretching along the horizon, framed by large winter trees stricken of leaves. I could be back home in the Midwest, traveling on the Illinois Central with my family, passing through the fields of southern Illinois for a visit to my grandmother's house. So many people all over the world, I think, and so many in these little towns, where they live and die and are known only to each other, their loved ones, and their families, and the bond between townspeople is etched into sidewalks and streets with strong and lasting foundation. The train is becoming crowded now, with groups of two or three children boarding at a time, book bags and chatter, they must have just got off school, and there are older people, too, with briefcases and trench coats, the uniform of white collar workers the world over.

Very quickly, the seat next to me is taken up by a man named Gunther, which I know to be true because he immediately introduces himself. Gunther has dirty blonde hair, curly and slightly receding, countered by sharp blue eyes. He wears a big wooly sweater and khaki pants and looks a lot like a fellow named Theodore who I met the year before in Nairn, a little town on the Moray Firth in Scotland. Theodore is an expat from Minneapolis who lives in Inverness, he married a Scottish girl and his smile and he shares hair, eye, and sweater styles with Gunther. Certain people you meet once you never forget them, other folks you share intimate moments with of one kind or another and they quickly recede into the grey mist of time.

When Gunther sits down, it's not with an overbearing "I'm going to distract you from your book and start babbling and telling you all about myself in a self-confessional fashion" manner; it's with a quiet certainty and polite respect. And, so, not surprisingly, instead of shutting myself up tight, I lower my book and begin to chat. Very quickly I learn that Gunther has two daughters, that he is heading back home to Berlin, where he lives. He spends four days a week working and living in Hannover, away from his family, and then he goes back to see them each long weekend (and holiday) in Berlin. I say this must be difficult, and he says it is, but then shrugs and tells me the money is good. We talk about the Wall, the state provided education and health care his children get, his love of Frank Zappa's music, and the impending war in Iraq. This will be a running theme for the rest of this tour, people asking me my opinion on the impending war in Iraq. People don't think we're all as crazy as our president, but they want to ask someone who might calm their fears assuredly. Fortunately, for me, and them, I am one of those people. I oppose the war wholeheartedly and after commiserating on its folly, we move on to other topics.

The train lets me off at my destination, Zoo Station, appropriately located at the world-famous Berlin Zoo. It is also well-known for being a magnet for homeless people and junkies. The escalator takes me up to a landing that is part of a tunnel whereby I have two directions to choose. I'm not sure what side of the station to get out of, and I go forward, stepping onto a poorly lit sidewalk next to a mission, where a homeless woman begins jabbering at me in German and waving newspapers in my direction. I assume this is the equivalent of the papers homeless folks sell on the street in New York or Chicago, to earn something close to a living wage and the illusion of respect. My heart and feet are tired from my journey, however, so I simply nod my head and say, "No sprechen de Deutsche," a phrase that I will repeat several times over the course of my journey, though I will remember this woman's determined look for days.

I retrace my steps and exit the other side of the tunnel where I'm immediately awash in a wave of honking horns and colored lights, which cut through the cold and silent darkness and give my drooping eyes a welcome buzz, urging them to open wider. It is New York, it is Chicago, it is London, it is all the big cities in the world I've been to and loved. There is movement, energy, and people everywhere. I feel, immediately, as close to home as I have since I left Nashville. I'm mood swinging now, from down to up, from longing for sleep to ready to roam. I find a phone booth and call my host, get directions, and proceed to hail a cab.

"Uh, Xantener Str. 5, Wilmersdorf," I read from a printed e-mail, as I slide into the back seat.

My cabbie looks in the rear view mirror and smiles as we pull away from the cab stand. "Hello, Mr. London," he says, "you are my first fare of the day!"

"Let's celebrate," I reply.

He laughs heartily.

I ask him how late into the night his shift goes and if he is a Berliner. It turns out his family is from Turkey, but he has been in Berlin since he was a small child. I've had Turkish coffee before, at this great falafel joint near University of Chicago, but other than that, I wouldn't know a thing about Turkey or Turkish ways, so I don't pretend otherwise. He asks me where I came in from and I told him Chicago, though I presently live in Nashville.

"So you are American?" he says, with surprise in his voice. "But, where are you really from?"

"What do you mean?"

"Where is your family from, comprendo, mister?"

"Oh," I respond, "well, my dad's side is from the Netherlands, but my mom's side is Lithuania, going way back."

Then he smiles and I see him in the rear-view mirror again, while I'm nearly knocked onto the floor as we take another narrow city curve. "Well, then, you are not really American, man, why do you say you are American, when you are from here and there?"

I give him an answer I'd honed from many trips overseas.

"It depends on where I am. When I'm in the Netherlands, I'm Dutch, when I'm in the States, I'm an American."

This cracks him up, and he slaps the dash with one hand, shaking the St. Christopher statue like a crazy margarita. Even Turkish cab drivers in Berlin have St. Christophers on their dash.

"You are right, that is true," he continues. "I am Turkish and German, no I am Turkish and a Berliner, that is what I am."

At this point, the cab driver tells me a little bit about his brothers and sisters, and his wife and family and before I know it, we are pulling up to my host's place. There is a light on beyond the door, and in a minute, my friend Tom comes bounding down the steps. My cabbie opens up the trunk as I get out of the car. "Let me help you with your bags, Mr. American." Then, he turns to Tom and laughs again, speaking in German. I pay him for the fare and watch him drive away as Tom looks on.

"I don't know what you said to that guy, but he thought you were really great."

Tom grew up in upstate New York, lived in Nashville for awhile, toured Europe and met a girl from Berlin, who he married and had a child with. He has been there 18 years, and he produces and records other people's music, does his own thing, and hosts a songwriter's night twice a month, which I'll be playing the following day. We walk through the courtyard and up the lift and into Tom and his family's spacious apartment. The air in the courtyard is cold and clear and carries the scent of detergent and fresh hanging laundry, a strange combination of smell that I notice every time I cross the pond. Upstairs, Tom and his wife and pre-school daughter invite me to sit down with them and share some homemade pizza. They are lovely, and though I'm tired from my long journey, they help me stay focused and awake. I'm on a desperate mission to beat jet lag and so I must stay awake until my new bedtime. After dinner, Tom takes me over to his dentist's apartment, where I have been graciously offered a place to stay.

The dentist's name is Wolfgang and the apartment is located in a large corner building overlooking Sybelstrasse, just down the block from the Kurfurstendamm, the main shopping district of Western Berlin. As I walk through the doorway, I'm given the choice of taking an endless row of stairs and landings that wind up all the way up to the fifth floor, or the lift, which can house maybe three people. It must have been hell moving in there, I think.

Upstairs, Wolfgang's digs resemble something out of a coffee table book on Bahaus Organic. It is cluttered yet sleek, traditional and yet modern. The vestibule empties into a main living room, where a giant harp and grand piano dominate the space, though they are set off to one side by the sliding rooftop door. Vintage guitars line the walls, along with pictures of Wolfgang in his various bands. There is also a couch and a large bed facing a widescreen plasma television that sits in the middle of the room.

Behind the television set, there's a spiral staircase that leads up to a walkway that crosses over to a home recording studio and makes you feel like a Vegas performer as you walk across and look down at what you imagine will be crowds of people coming and going. And, while they aren't crowds, there are people coming and going, because it seems like there are endless rooms in this apartment, with an endless series of borders, Pieter the flamenco singer, Braga, his manager, and Jacques, the man in a terrycloth bathrobe battling the sniffles. "I would love to talk," he says, upon introduction, "but I have a cold," waving his hands so I don't shake one, before scurrying back into his room.

Recovering in Berlin—Saturday, January 25, 2003

I sleep pretty well at Wolfgang's, only waking up once or twice not knowing where the hell I am, which is good for me on a night after a transatlantic trip. It is a comfortable guest room, my quarters. There is an alcove to one side attached to the main part of the room, and inside the nook an old antique typewriter sits on a plain wooden table. No paper scrolled inside, no fountain pens lying about, just a bare and lonesome typewriter, beckoning someone to call up the spirits of Goethe. My bed is a couch with a roll away mattress inside, but it has no springs, so it pulls out rather than rolls. Since no one stays here regularly, I can drop my stuff anywhere, take up space, and not have to worry about getting too organized or picking up after myself. Jacques' room is next door and occasionally I hear him sneezing and sniffling, but for the most part, it's very quiet. I'm down a hall from the main living room and kitchen.

Pieter, Braga, and Wolfgang have graciously offered to show me around the city, so I get up late enough to be rested, but early enough to stay on schedule and get some quality sightseeing in. After my shower, I get dressed and join the men; they're sitting around a breakfast nook in a corner beneath a large television that sits on a swivel arm. It seems like everything in Wolfgang's apartment sits on swivel arms, his television set, his computer screen, his guitar. I half-expect his head to swivel around at me when he's speaking. Bread, fruit, and coffee are laid out on the table, in abundance.

Pieter is from Koln, but he is half-Canadian and has spent a lot of time in America, so we hit it off pretty well. He is also a more-or-less working musician, like myself, and is more intimately familiar with that gig, although since he favors modern jazz, his artistic sensibilities and talents are much different than mine. Wolfgang is pleasant, but guarded, and he seems to enjoy very little, except speaking cryptically. Telling me about his failed marriage to a Filipino woman, he raises his sad eyes and says, "it was gambling," with a slight upturn at the end of the phrase, as if to test the air for a follow-up question. I say nothing, and no details follow. Braga has very good, quiet positive energy, but doesn't say much. He strikes me as a polite but formal man, well-dressed with fastidiously pressed sports jacket and carefully combed hair, and I later learn he used to be an architect before devoting himself to managing Pieter's music career. I think of the teacher in the *The Blue Angel* and weep for us all.

Pieter claims the role of tour guide and off we go in Wolfgang's elegant Mercedes complete with a talking map that tells us how to maneuver the streets as he drives down the Bismarkstrasse toward the Brandenberg Gate. Traffic is heavy like in any big city, but it is not impossible, we don't get stuck in any jams, and the drivers appear to be quite disciplined and orderly. The cars are smaller and many people ride scooters, shooting in and out of traffic effortlessly. Occasionally I spot a yellow Doppeldecker bus haltingly starting and stopping.

The Bismarkstrasse turns into the Strasse des 17 Juni and it is instantly familiar to me. I've seen Nazis marching down this corridor in endless miles of old World War II footage. The boulevard soon circles around the statue known as the Siegessaule, a column with a golden angel on the top, also recognizable, this time from Wim Wenders' seminal *Wings of Desire* film. My guide book says this is now a spot for gay cruising, and one gets a sense of layers of time circling, imprinting, and eventually erasing, the past. We park down by the Gate, and proceed to stroll around a square which bordered by foreign embassies, flags of other nations flying on the top of buildings. Rodin's "The Thinker" sits in the middle of the square, accompanied by an accordionist with a derby hat and black vest, playing sad German songs. We walk past him, and under the Brandenberg gate, across to the grounds of the Reichstag.

It's about 40 degrees Fahrenheit, not bad for a January day, and I'm dressed warmly with leather jacket and gloves. The wind is occasionally brisk and as Pieter takes my picture in front of the Reichstag, my eyes tear. Walking up to the Reichstag, I think of my father in World War II, riding through bombed-out Berlin on the back of a supply truck. I notice the bright modernistic globe that has been added, capping off the building's Romanesque base as if to symbolize the act of both rejecting and embracing history. We walk around the grounds silently. I see a black granite sculpture, a series of slabs in a row on the grounds, memorializing the concentration camp dead. Across the street there are crosses on a fence, memorializing those who died going over the wall; around the corner, local Muslims gather for a peace protest. And, not far from all this, there is construction going on for a new monument memorializing the Holocaust dead—it is near the site of Hitler's bunker. These are an intense collision of images, so concentrated that I feel slightly uncomfortable taking pictures or having my picture taken.

Pieter breaks the silence to provide some native perspective. "I understand what Churchill did, he should have done it, it was too much, but he had to do it." He's talking about the bombings, as the war was winding down, the bombings that devastated cities like Dresden and Berlin. Pieter's response, I'll learn, seems to be pretty typical, that most Germans feel they deserved it, and that they must never forget what happened, but they also must move on. Later, as we get to know each other a little, I'll ask how they feel about the constant representation of Nazi's in Hollywood movies and all that old cinematic footage we revisit on a daily basis on cable television. Braga responds by saying, "They should be shown, but every culture has its shame, like the Indians in America." I learn that Braga is a big fan of Navajo culture and I tell him about the great Tony Hillerman mystery books, which he is unfamiliar with.

As we stand in front of the Reichstag, Wolfgang begins to complain about the cold. We decide to head over to the Hotel Aldon for espresso, the Aldon being a beautiful old regal hotel built in 1907 and reopened to all of Berlin since unification. Everyone from Charlie Chaplin to Lawrence of Arabia stayed there, the hotel flyers brag, and we're all in for a treat because Wolfgang has insisted that he'll buy our coffees. Pieter starts slipping in and out of a campy impersonation of Chancellor Willy Schroeder as we stroll back across the main square. Mr. Schroeder is currently gaining a lot of favor with German citizens for his No War in Iraq stance. Of course, while I agree with his position, it has its own political currency in Germany and Schroeder is aware of this.

We enter the lobby of the Aldon, and Pieter continues to impersonate the Chancellor, this time in a quieter, stilted formal voice. "For the first time in my life, I'm proud to be German," he says. Then, he smiles, quickly. "Actually, Doog, a bartender said that to me, but see it is very important, this feeling, people here have had enough of the wars." Seeing all this, it is ironic that just a couple days before my arrival, U.S. Defense Secretary Donald Rumsfeld was quoted as saying the Germans don't understand their history. After I left Berlin, the protests would intensify, and the avenues formerly filled with stormtroopers would be filled with record numbers of Germans calling for peace. Political capital or not, that made an impression on me.

Later that afternoon, as dusk begins to fall and shadows blanket the antique instruments in Wolfgang's apartment, he treats me to some of his flamenco guitar playing. He's really quite good as a player, but it is quite strange for me to hear these Django Reinhardt-inspired compositions coming from his lips, sung completely in German. Apparently, Wolfgang used to lead a band called Ikarus, they made a couple records, even did a film score—and as mentioned, pictures of him and his band hang everywhere in the apartment. He also has his guitar rigged with what appeared to be a very expensive wireless set up that allows him to both sing and play while walking around the kitchen.

"Music is life!" He shouts to me, as he picks. I think he wanted to me to unpack my guitar and jam, but I was content to watch this slight man, grey goatee and neatly combed hair, dance around his kitchen, filling the room with German flamenco. Wolfgang tells me how he invented the wireless contraption, to allow Ikarus to play restaurants, different members walking from table to table while they played. I silently wonder how settling that would be to the digestion system. Suddenly, Wolfgang stops playing and abruptly hangs his guitar among a half dozen hanging next to the breakfast nook. His body collapses on the seat across from me, like a marionette at the end of a show, and he gazes sadly out the window as pigeons land on the roof.

"But, you see, I was never professional . . . I could only play part-time."

I nod.

"I grew up in Leipzig, in the former East Germany," he adds. "My father, he wanted me to have a trade, and my gift is my hands," he says, holding them out for me to see. "And so I became a dentist."

I wonder what he is so sad about, I mean, he has a Mercedes, a great apartment, all kinds of guitars, a grand piano in his living room, a TV set bigger than my apartment, and he lives in one of the coolest neighborhoods, in what is one of the world's coolest cities. Granted, his marriage broke up because of gambling, but still, he has it better than most.

"You see, people didn't take me seriously. I became known as the singing dentist."

I admit that might be hard to take, but again, I think of all the vacations he told me he'd taken, the short work week, the musical opportunities he has enjoyed. There is a wash of silence come over us, however, and so I let that silence be. After what seems like a reasonable amount of time, I ask him if I could use his internet to check in with my wife Molly back home. He sets me up, and to be polite, but also for real, I ask if I can have his e-mail address so I can stay in touch once I got back to the States. He hands me a business card.

Wolfgang's card bears his name and address, a musical staff, and instead of notes on the staff, there are caricatures of little smiling bicuspids and molars playing a melody.

That night is my first gig of the tour, an "in-the-round" hosted by my new friend Tom. For the uninitiated, in-the-rounds are where everyone sits in a circle and one guitar slinger plays a song, followed by the person on their right, and the person on their right and so on, going around in a circle. There are four individuals and it means you usually wind up playing five songs while spending the rest of the time with a smile on your face, looking at the person next to you while they play, thinking about what you're going to play next or what you're going to be doing after the show. My in-the-round partners are Tom, the host, a woman from California named Gail who usually plays as a duo with her daughter, and a funny guy named Klaus who speaks and sings everything in robust German, complete with crazy arm gestures and faces, often stopping playing altogether to launch into an animated cabaret-inspired monologue. I don't understand a word, but the audience is roaring and so do I, because he reminds me of Monty Python's Michael Palin.

In a twist on the format, they have an open chair where members of the audience can come up and sit in for a tune. Pieter, Braga, and Wolfgang come down to catch the set, and Tom, the host, "coaxes" Wolfgang into playing a song. It so happens that Wolfgang has brought his guitar with him, the one with the wireless electronic set-up that probably cost more money than our car back home. However, when he plugs it in, there is no sound. The sound man hurries over, fiddles with the cord and gets nothing; there's probably a short in the jack. He disappears into the back room and comes out with an extra mike and stand and sets them up in front of Wolfgang's guitar. It doesn't take that long, but in comparison to the way the show has been going, the amount of dead air in the room is painful. People begin to mutter and glasses clink that much louder than normal. Luckily, Wolfgang recovers and salvages his spot.

As for me, I wasn't sure how I'd go over with the language barrier and all, but people respond in all the right places, and as I circulate through the audience, I meet folks from California, Massachusetts, New York, and London, as well as Berliners, east and west, and some folks from the Czech Republic. It's a good night. I get back to Wolfgang's and into bed by 3:30 or so.

Absorbing Berlin—Sunday, January 26, 2003

I rarely spend two days in one place on tour, but as it was my first visit to Berlin, I intentionally scheduled an extra day to explore this new place. I rise around 10 a.m. and join the men for bread, fruit, and coffee, because, as I've quickly learned, there's nothing like fruit and coffee to get your day going. I add my road-vitamin routine—about 6,000 mg of C, 400 of E, and a multi-vitamin with iron that's so loaded it's advertised as for those "over 60." I cough a few times. "Are you sick, Doog?" Pieter asks, as I pile more vitamins into my body.

Pieter is very kind the whole time I am in Berlin, making sure I am seeing everything I want to see, know where everything is, have enough fruit and coffee at my disposal, and so on. As he warms up over the weekend, he starts playing me tracks from his records and I find that he is an amazing singer in an Al Jarreau kind of way and an even more fluid flamenco player than Wolfgang. For some reason, both of them favor gut-string classical guitars. Although I initially wondered about Pieter's relationship with Braga, I soon find out it is strictly professional. I detest stereotypes, you know, but Pieter's hair is cut short and fastidiously groomed, he likes wearing baseball caps and designer jeans, and he used to live in San Francisco and loves to talk about his adventures there, not that there is anything wrong with any of that.

Pieter is also impressed with my newfound fatherhood and at one point, after I speak of my little son back home, he becomes reflective.

"Family, yes, that is soo important, Doog." He always called me Doog. "I had my days when I experimented sexually, but I would like a family," he adds, in a stark matter-of-fact tone.

Artists are always sussing each other out on a creative level, and my instinct was that Pieter will hate my music; it is so different from his. But, he asks to swap CDs on the basis of what he heard the night before. He begins speaking about my music and comments, thoughtfully, "Yes, I can see, the story is very important, ahhhh, yes." He smiles, taking in the cubist cover of my latest effort. "Perhaps, too, one day you will write a book."

Here it is, Pieter!

Anyway, to begin our adventures, Pieter wants to take us to the train station that I'll be leaving from the next day, so he'll know how to find it. Braga, Pieter, Wolfgang, and I all pile into the Mercedes again, like a motley German-American version of a Beatles cartoon, and head back up the boulevard, past the Reichstag and the former Soviet Embassy, turning east onto Karl Marx Allee. We're met with a stunning view as we travel down this expansive palisade, about six cars wide, bordered on each side by row after row of huge apartment complexes, drab block buildings like those I've seen in *Dr. Zhivago* or *Reds*. At this point, I am beginning to realize that many of my preconceptions of Germany and the eastern bloc countries, in particular, have been shaped by film and pop culture. If the film exchange holds true, I can only imagine what they think of my hometowns of Chicago and Nashville. We see vendors selling Cossacks on folding tables on the sidewalk and Braga dryly remarks, "We are in Moscow, gentlemen."

After we find Ostbanhof Station, we circle back to Postdammer Platz to see a bit of the new rebuilt Berlin, including the famous Jahn-designed Sony building. It's an amazing space, all glass and broad angles, rising to the sky, and both Braga and I stand in admiration. Talk of architecture gives us something to connect on, for as a Chicagoan, I grew up in a city bespeckled with Sullivan, Frank Lloyd Wright, Jahn, and Van der Rohe, among others. Then we are whisked off to the Einstein Café for strudel and espresso, which gives me a taste of the Brecht-Weill prewar Berlin. The Café is an old artist's haunt, newspapers from around the world hanging on big wooden sticks by the door, while couples walk in for their morning pastries and coffee, delivered by an endless array of waiters scuffling around in white aprons and hats. If I lived in Berlin, I'd probably be there every Sunday. The food is excellent, and everyone is in good spirits, except for Wolfgang who complains about the poor service, although he does pay for the strudels.

Wolfgang says he is tired and ready for a nap, so we drop him back at the flat and then continue on to Charlottenburg Castle, the former home of King Frederick I of Prussia, or the Great Elector, if you're in need of a nickname. Freddie's statue looms over the courtyard like an elderly relative, overseeing expansive grounds filled with majestic buildings, important monuments, and long walkways of trees and gardens.

The main building, or Castle itself, dates back to 1695 and is so huge (and expensive to tour), that we decide to simply walk the grounds a bit, turning up our collars to fight the sharp winds. I imagine trees and flowers blooming splendidly in summer. There is a vendor outside playing classical music on a harpsichord, for tips, a little Beethoven on ice.

"Ah, Frederick," Braga muses to the strains of the "Moonlight Sonata," "there was a man."

From the Castle, it is on to another café, where Braga also expresses his admiration for John F. Kennedy. "There was a man," he says again. "I'll always remember his great speech 'Iche bien Berliner.' I do not like to admit it, because it shows I am old, but I was there." Braga grows pensive, and nearly teary-eyed, as he reminisces. I try to head back in time with him and see him in the crowd as a young man, hanging on the words of our president. I see him wrapped up in wool coat, bracing the wind with a loved one on his arm, their future of possibilities encapsulated in a few simple words of hope and imagination. It is a bit much for me, and so I ask Braga if the myth about the jelly doughnuts is true.

He chuckles and nods his head. "It does not matter, does it?"

Then, Pieter and I talk about music, and somehow the conversation lands on Wolfgang.

"You know, Doog, Wolfgang is great," Pieter says, "He is a dear friend, but he always says 'music is life.' Music is work! When I am done, and I get home, I do not want to play, I want to rest. See, you understand this, Doog, you are out playing."

Pieter drains his espresso. I ask him about "the gambling."

"Oh, that was his wife, she gambled his money away. Sad, really."

When we get back to the flat, Wolfgang is still lying in bed in the middle of the living room, covers pulled up to his chin. He is watching an episode of *Star Trek Voyager*, dubbed in German, on the huge television screen in front of him. Captain Janeway greets Tupac on the bridge with a cheery "Gutentag." We rouse Wolfgang from his half-slumber, and together we all walk down to the Kurfurstendamm for Chinese food.

"You know, Doog," Pieter says, "that guy from *Hogan's Heroes* used to live in this neighborhood, the actor."

"Really?" I'm not sure if he is talking about Col. Klink or Sergeant Schultz, but I don't want to ask. Maybe he was even thinking of LaBeau.

Braga is quiet. Wolfgang doesn't complain about anything, but he may still be sleepy. This time, however, I pay.

That night, when I go to bed, I hear house music throbbing through the walls, somewhere on Wolfgang's block, if not in his building. After reading a little while, I put Miles Davis' masterpiece *Kind of Blue* into my Discman to distract myself from the steady, though distant pounding. I focus on Miles' beautiful blue notes and think of lying in the dark and listening to this music with my wife and newborn son not too many months before. Not surprisingly, I nod off quickly and sleep the sound and dreamless sleep of the dead.

Leaving Berlin—Monday, January 27, 2003

On my last morning in Berlin, Wolfgang and I are having a leisurely fruit and coffee breakfast when he begins asking me about the forthcoming gigs in Saxony. In the midst of our conversation, he flat-out asks me how much money I'm going to be making. I am taken aback, tell the truth, and he responds with what could be classified as shock.

"This is impossible!? That much? How can this be? Why, Pieter, he had a big hit with that song "East West Tokyo L.A." and he doesn't make that much!"

Wolfgang has been a most gracious host to me, welcoming a total stranger into his home. Nevertheless, I still don't know how to respond because I never know how to respond in these situations. I'm never quite sure of where the line of defense ends and the line of defensiveness begins. Wolfgang's inference, of course, is that I am far inferior to Pieter (and himself) musically and there is an injustice in my Saxony success to come. But, I must admit, my feeling is that on one hand, there isn't much of a market for German flamenco; and on the other hand, Wolfgang really isn't out there hustling it and doesn't understand the chain of events triggered by my CD release which led to a copy of said disc falling into the hand of Thomas of Affalter, the German promoter who liked the music and booked the shows. Thomas did this because he is a fan of American, Canadian, and British singer-songwriters and because he likes my work. "Your music gives me quiet in a noisy world," he told me via e-mail. "It sounds like you wrote a fairytale, circumstanced with music." The bottom line is, if you do good work and keep pushing, good things happen, although the nature of those good things may be slightly different than what you imagined.

On a more practical point, I was only playing a week of shows in Saxony and even if Wolfgang fit the circuit, he wouldn't be able to play the market very often before it became saturated with flamenco. Do I sound defensive yet? I try, in calm tones, to sum up these ideas for Wolfgang's benefit. But, as I do, he appears to be even more dumfounded, and frankly, outraged. I could see years of lost choices swimming behind his eyes, perhaps he shouldn't have been a dentist, perhaps he should've thrown himself into his music instead, if hack songwriters like this American could make that much money. And, I wouldn't argue about choices, but you know that's why you pick one thing or the other—you can't have it both ways. And sometimes when folks try to have it all, they wind up with nothing.

Later, on the way to our train station, I tell Pieter about this breakfast conversation.

"Oh, that's Wolfgang, Doog; he's always trying to size things up. You know, he didn't go out and what do you say, ummmm . . ." He pauses, searching for the colloquialism, "go for it, so now he regrets this. It's sad really. But, he doesn't know how it is."

Pieter is right. Lots of people don't know how it is.

Inside Ostenhaf Station, back in East Berlin, I make my way to the ticket counter and it soon becomes clear that I am in a land where very little English is spoken. The older woman at the counter goes to fetch a young man, and since he is of this new generation, he is able to help me. After that, I still have time to kill, so I go over to a kiosk in the middle of the station, next to a giant yellow porcelain bear, and buy a toy Dopperdecker bus for my son. I also get a latte and a jelly doughnut—it's much smaller than the ones back home, and not as gooey, but it's the first one I've seen since I've arrived in Berlin. It's also a fitting snack for the ride out of town.

My train pulls up right on time, 10:30 a.m., another sleek shiny train with quiet doors and whispering people, sitting in twos and threes, crowded into the aisles. I sit on my guitar case in the vestibule and stare through the glass doors at terrain that is grittier and seemingly much poorer than what I've noticed in the western half of the country. The stations we pass on the way to Zwickau are often dilapidated and worn. People's eyes are heavier, their skin more weather-beaten, it's as if everything had turned sepia and I was looking into old photographs of my immigrant grandparents as they trekked through Lithuania.

I'd learned through my travels that many West Germans looked at unification with mixed feelings because it took the resources and taxes from their half of the country and spread them thinner among a greater population. But the easterners looked at unification as life reborn. I finish my doughnut and think about Kennedy. Later that evening, as I settle into my digs in Affalter, Thomas's wife Christiane says something to me that I'll never forget. A woman about fifty, with two grown children and a new career in front of her, she looked at me with a gleam in her eye and said, "You have to understand, until a few years ago, we didn't think our lives could change."